CRIME BITERS!

DOG DAY AFTERSCHOOL

TOMMY GREENWALD
WITH ILLUSTRATIONS BY ADAM STOWER

| SCHOLASTIC PRESS | NEW YORK

FOR
DUGAN—THE BALLER
MARA—THE WRITER
EDEN—THE FIGHTER

Text copyright © 2017 by Tommy Greenwald
Illustrations copyright © 2017 by Adam Stower

Library of Congress Cataloging-in-Publication Data available

ISBN 978-0-545-78402-3

10 9 8 7 6 5 4 3 2 1   17 18 19 20 21

Printed in the U.S.A.   23
First edition, October 2017

Book design by Yaffa Jaskoll

MEET THE GANG!
(IN CASE YOU HAVEN'T MET US BEFORE)

PROFILE UPDATE

Name: Jimmy Bishop
Age: 11
Occupation: President and Founder, CrimeBiters
Interests: Solving crime, protecting society, Daisy Flowers

PROFILE UPDATE

Name: Irwin Wonk
Age: 11
Occupation: Best Friend and Cofounder of the CrimeBiters
Interests: Questioning everything I do

PROFILE UPDATE

Name: Daisy Flowers
Age: Just turned 11
Occupation: Cofounder of
the CrimeBiters
Interests: Amazingly
enough, wanting to hang
around with us

PROFILE UPDATE

Name: Baxter Bratford
Age: 12
Occupation: CrimeBiter
Interests: Trying to ma[k]
everyone forget he use[d]
to be a bully

AN EXTREMELY BRIEF HISTORY OF THE CRIMEBITERS

Case File #1: The Bad Babysitter

Jimmy Bishop adopts a dog, Abby. He soon realizes that she's a crime-fighting superhero vampire dog. Jimmy forms the CrimeBiters with his best friend, Irwin Wonk, his new crush—I mean friend—Daisy Flowers, and of course Abby. Together, they solve the Case of the Bad Babysitter and help catch the perpetrators, Barnaby Bratford and his sister, the evil Mrs. Cragg. Then they make friends with Barnaby's son, the former bully Baxter Bratford, and he becomes the fifth CrimeBiter.

Case File #2: The Rotten Rival

Jimmy's parents make Abby go to obedience school, where she becomes much better behaved, but also more like other dogs. Jimmy doesn't like that very much. Jimmy joins the lacrosse team. Irwin doesn't like that very much. Daisy makes a new friend named Mara. Jimmy and Irwin don't like that very much. Baxter is on the lacrosse team too, but Jimmy quickly becomes better than him. Baxter doesn't like that very much. Then a bunch of kids on the team start getting hurt, and no one likes that very much. Luckily, the CrimeBiters discover someone is trying to hurt the kids on purpose, solve the Case of the Rotten Rival, and save the day—and everyone likes that very, very much.

Oh, and Mrs. Cragg turns out to be nice.

Go figure!

INTRODUCTION

HEY, YOU GUYS.

Haven't seen you in a while. How have you been?

I've been pretty good: the school year is winding down, and things have been busy, with homework, friends, extracurricular activities—the usual stuff.

Oh, and Abby saved the day again.

You know, Abby, my crime-fighting superhero vampire dog?

Yeah, her.

She single-handedly (make that single-pawedly) foiled another villainous plot that threatened our very way of life.

Okay, okay, that's a slight exaggeration. She had a little help, after all, from Irwin, Daisy, Baxter, and myself—we call ourselves the CrimeBiters.

Oh, wait. There was one other person.

Well, not a person, exactly.

A cat.

But I'm jumping ahead. I don't want to ruin the ending!

So let's go all the way back to the beginning.

Three weeks ago.

PART ONE

THE FURRY FRIEND

CHAPTER 1

"SPIN!" I HOLLERED. "Weave! Crouch! Lean!"

Abby spun, weaved, crouched, and leaned.

We were in the middle of a training session in the backyard, and it was time to increase the pressure. I took the giant stuffed panda bear I won at a fair ringtoss two years earlier (it was a pretty lucky shot, I'll admit) and held it over my head.

"Bad guy! Attack! Attack!"

Now, it may have had a little something to do with the peanut butter I smeared on the panda's face, but Abby jumped so high I swear I thought she was going to leap over the house! She ripped the panda from my hands and started shaking it like crazy. Its adorable black nose popped off in two seconds, and three seconds after that, stuffing was flying all over the backyard.

"Stand down!" I hollered. "Suspect apprehended! Stand down!"

Abby stopped, released the panda from her death grip, and started licking peanut butter off the stuffed animal's mangled left ear.

"That wasn't such a great idea," I muttered to myself, already regretting the decision to have Abby attack the biggest thing I'd ever won in my entire life. "Don't eat that!" I said to Abby, as she started examining the panda's insides. "It's not turkey stuffing. It's stuffed animal stuffing."

The screen door opened.

"Jimmy! What's going on out here?"

I looked up to see my dad standing there with a wooden spoon in his hand. That meant he was cooking something—never a good idea.

"Hey, Dad. Just, uh, running through some training exercises with Abby."

"Training exercises?"

"Yeah, you know—"

"I know, I know," my dad said, waving the spoon in my general direction. "Well, I appreciate all you're doing for society, but let's clean that mess up and call it a day. Oh, by the way, we're having asparagus omelets for dinner."

"Asparagus omelets?" I moaned.

FACT: The words *asparagus* and *omelet* should never be used in the same sentence.

"Yup," my dad said, grinning. "Good, and good *for* you!"

He went back inside, and I looked down at Abby, who had moved on to the panda's right ear.

"Hey, can I get some of that peanut butter?" I asked.

She ignored me.

CHAPTER 2

"JIMMY?" SAID MY dad.

I pushed the omelet around the plate and didn't look up. Whenever my dad said "Jimmy?" like that, it usually didn't lead to good things.

"Yeah?"

"Let's talk about the summer. There's only a few weeks left in the school year, and we should get it settled."

Oh boy. I had my whole summer planned out in my head, and it wasn't really up for discussion.

"What about it?" I asked.

My big sister, Misty, who *loved* asparagus omelets, grinned with excitement. "I am so psyched for the summer! Jarrod invited me to drive across the country with his family!" Jarrod Knight is Misty's boyfriend, and he's actually a really nice guy, as long as you don't hold his questionable taste in girls against him.

My dad raised his eyebrows. "Excuse me?"

"Yup, they're renting a big mobile home thingy!" she announced. "Sounds great, right?"

"Uh, yeah, other than the fact that if you think you're going, you're completely crazy," said my dad. "Do Jarrod's parents have any clue about this invitation?"

"Er," said Misty, which I think is another word for *no*.

Headlights flashed across the living room, which was Abby's cue to run over to the front door and start wagging her tail like crazy. She likes to greet every family member like a warrior returning from battle.

This time, it was my mom, getting home from work. "Easy, girl," she said, giving Abby a hug. "Easy." Mom and Abby had had a few run-ins in the past, which usually involved a chewed-up item of expensive clothing, but they were good pals now.

After several jumps where her head almost scraped the ceiling, Abby decided the greeting could end. My mom sat down at the table, and my dad picked up where he left off.

"Misty wants to spend the summer driving across America in a giant trailer with Jarrod and his family."

My mom's eyes went wide, then narrowed down to little slits. "Over my dead body," she said.

"Mom!" Misty whined, in full drama-queen mode. "I'm going to be a junior in high school! I'm practically an adult!"

"I totally think you should let her go," I said, but not out of brotherly love or anything. I was just thinking about getting Misty's bedroom for the summer— it's about three times bigger than mine.

"See?" Misty said, grabbing on to my uncharacteristic generosity as if it were a life raft. "Even Jimmy says I should get to go!"

"You're not going," said my mom, with an *end of discussion* tone of voice. Misty slumped back in her seat, while Mom turned her attention to me.

"What about you? Time to start thinking about summer plans, right?"

"I have it all figured out," I told her, hoping she would accept that and just move on.

"Oh yeah?" Mom asked. "Like what?"

"Oh, mostly CrimeBiters stuff," I said. I looked down at Abby, kind of wishing she would do something distracting like eat one of my mom's shoes, but she was busy running in her sleep.

FACT: Dogs run in their sleep more than most people run awake.

"I'm also going to keep volunteering at Shep's shelter," I added. Shep Lansing ran the Northport Animal Rescue Foundation—which is where we got Abby—and I helped him out three days a week after school, feeding the dogs, cleaning up, and doing other odd jobs. "Plus, I want to go to lacrosse camp, and make sure I read everything on the summer reading list for school, stuff like that."

"Good plan," said my mom.

"Sounds like a great summer," my dad chimed in.

I stared at them both in shock. "Really? I can just . . . kind of do what I want?"

My mom kissed my cheek. "Or less," she said. "Sometimes it seems like you take on too much, and we just want you to have fun. Summer is a time to relax, right? No stress."

She turned back to my sister. "So, should we talk about your summer, and what you might *actually* do, instead of running off with your boyfriend?"

"NO!" said Misty, who then got up from the table and ran up the stairs, went into her bedroom (which was much bigger than mine, did I mention that?), and slammed the door.

"Jeez, what's her problem?" I muttered, but I was giggling inside.

I take back everything bad I ever said about big sisters.

They really come in handy sometimes.

CHAPTER 3

THE NEXT DAY was Saturday, which meant one thing: our weekly CrimeBiters meeting! By the time Abby and I got to the Boathouse, my friend and fellow CrimeBiter Baxter Bratford was already there, but he wasn't doing either of his two usual activities—eating something chocolate, or sleeping.

Instead, he was hunched over a notebook, scribbling away like a madman.

Abby went over to say hi, which meant plopping herself in Baxter's lap and refusing to get up until he started petting her.

"Whatcha doing?" I asked Baxter.

He sighed so deeply, he almost fell over. "Ugh," he said, but I immediately knew what he meant.

FACT: Homework is such a scary concept that sometimes it's difficult to even utter the actual word.

"Seriously?" I said. "It's Saturday! What class?"

"I don't even know," Baxter muttered, but I knew that couldn't be true. Or could it? I knew Baxter wasn't exactly Albert Einstein, but I was pretty sure he could tell the difference between social studies and science.

Baxter suddenly flung the notebook down in frustration. "It's all so hard! I need a nap." He lay down on his back and closed his eyes, which was definitely a more natural position for him than crouched over a book. "My parents are really starting to get mad about my grades," he said. "They said I might have to go to summer school."

Now, this was a very surprising statement, but not in the way you might expect. Nope, it was surprising because Baxter said "parents." Meaning, mom *and dad*.

I hadn't heard him use that word since his dad had been put in jail, and that was almost a year ago.

FACT: To learn more about Barnaby Bratford and his jewelry-stealing crime ring, and how Baxter himself used to be a bully but later became my lacrosse teammate and part of our gang, please read the earlier CrimeBiters books. You can even read them right now if you want to! It's okay, I'll wait.

"Summer school? Yikes," I said, but before I could figure out what to say after that, I heard a high-pitched, lispy voice squeal, "What up, bros?"

That sound could only belong to one person.

Baxter and I looked at each other, rolled our eyes, and waited for our friend Irwin Wonk to climb the stairs to the roof.

"What did you just say?" I asked Irwin, as he stood there, huffing and puffing.

"Uh, what up, bros?" Irwin said, with a little less swagger this time.

Baxter got up from his pre-nap, walked over to Irwin, and put his hand on his shoulder. "Irwin? Can I tell you something? You're a lot of things—a lot of good things, even—but cool isn't one of them."

"Yeah," I agreed. "It's probably best you stay away from language like that."

"You know what?" Irwin said. "You guys are dorks."

"True," I said. "But we accept it."

"We own it," Baxter added.

"We embrace it," I finished, and Baxter and I started dancing around in a circle, chanting, "You're one of us!"— which may have been the dorkiest move of them all.

"Cut it out!" Poor Irwin. He was the very definition of nerdy, but he wasn't quite ready to give up on his dream of making it to the other side.

Irwin looked around, ready to change the subject. "Where's Daisy?"

Baxter and I stopped in our tracks. "Yeah, where is she?" we both wondered aloud. Daisy was never, ever late—which was one of the 4,392,955 good things about her.

As we were trying to figure out where Daisy could have been, Abby's tail suddenly shot skyward, as straight as a fishing pole.

"What is it, girl?" I said, but Abby didn't move. She looked like a statue, staring down toward the front door of the Boathouse.

"She must see something," Irwin suggested.

"Or smell something," I said.

"Something bad," Baxter added.

FACT: See previous fact.

Abby started slowly walking toward the door, and I heard a soft, low sound coming from deep inside of her. It was more of a rumble than a growl. It was a

sound that meant, *I sense danger. And danger makes me angry.*

We all got up and watched her. She cocked her head, and for some reason, Baxter and I cocked our heads too.

"What are you guys doing?" Irwin said. "You're not dogs."

We uncocked our heads.

Then a familiar voice said, "Sorry I'm late!"

"See, Abby?" said Baxter. "It's just Daisy. No big deal, right?"

Abby didn't answer though, because she was still on high alert.

"We're almost there!" Daisy added, which was a little confusing. *We're?*

Finally, I couldn't take it anymore. I ran to the door and threw it open, just as Daisy was about to open it herself from the other side.

"Hey, guys!" she said brightly. "What's up?"

Now, ordinarily, we all would have said, "Not much." But this was the opposite of ordinary. This was extremely *extra*ordinary. Because Daisy was holding something in her arms. And that something was alive.

"Oh, right!" she chirped, noticing our stares. "Where are my manners?" She thrust out her arms, so we could see the something-that-was-alive up close.

It was a cat.

"This is—" she began, but none of us could hear the rest, because that was when Abby started barking her head off.

CHAPTER 4

FACT: Cats and dogs don't get along at all. In fact, they usually fight like, well, cats and dogs.

"ABBY, STOP BARKING," I said. Then, louder: "ABBY, QUIET!" But it wasn't any use. She was yowling and howling and I was a little worried that she was going to leap one of her famous leaps and break out her famous fangs and clamp her jaw right down on that kitten's cute little head. But she didn't, probably because she loved Daisy, and was willing to give her the benefit of the doubt. Up to a point.

Finally, I fished a treat out of my backpack and gave it to Abby as a distraction, so the rest of us could find out a little more about our unexpected guest.

Irwin pointed at the little fur ball. "What *is* that?" he said, getting right to the point.

"This is my new cat!" Daisy said, with a giant smile on her face. "Her name is Purrkins! Get it? *PURR*-kins?" She nuzzled the cat's face with her own. "And she's *PURR*-fect!"

Abby didn't think Purrkins was *purr*-fect though—not by a long shot. Abby wasn't growling anymore, but she was eyeing the cat with a menacing stare.

"Oh, Abby," Daisy said, rolling her eyes. "Stop being so ridiculous. Purrkins is the sweetest little thing. You and her are going to be bestest buds!"

"Bestest buds?" I asked. "I don't know. Dogs don't generally like cats very much. And Abby doesn't like any animal until she gets to know them."

Daisy plopped down on one of the run-down old beach chairs that were still scattered around the abandoned boathouse. "That's why I brought her here! The sooner Purrkins and Abby become pals, the better! And how awesome will the CrimeBiters be with *two* pets instead of only one?"

Her choice of words offended me, for some reason. "Abby is not a pet," I said, even though that's exactly what she was.

"Wait, hold on," Irwin said to Daisy. "You want Purrkins to become part of our gang?"

PROFILE

Name: Purrkins

Age: Age isn't important for someone with nine lives

Occupation: Daisy's cat

Interests: Making Daisy happy, freaking Abby out

She laughed like that was the dumbest question ever. "Of course, silly!"

Baxter, who'd been sitting there minding his own business and pretending to study during this whole episode, finally cleared his throat. "Um, we should talk about this," he said quietly. "Abby has already proven herself a very capable CrimeBiter, even though she's not necessarily the superhero crime-fighting vampire dog Jimmy thinks she is."

They all looked at me. Baxter was right, I did think that. Wait, I take it back. I *knew* that. Just because no one else believed it doesn't mean it wasn't true.

"If you're saying that Purrkins has to prove herself, well, I accept that," Daisy said. "She is prepared to go through any exercise in order to show that she belongs in the gang."

"Where did you get her anyway?" I asked.

"Shep's shelter," answered Daisy. "She really needed a home."

My heart melted just a little bit. Shep's shelter was the most awesome place in the whole world.

"That's great," I said. I decided to be a good sport, and walked over to the cat. "Hey, Purrkins. I'm Jimmy, and I'm happy to meet you. You seem like a very nice little cat. Welcome to our clubhouse."

I reached out to pet the cat, ready to be greeted with a nice purr. I mean, it *was* half her name, right?

Yeah, well, it didn't work out that way.

As soon as I started petting her, Purrkins arched her back way up high to the sky. I saw her claws come out of her paws, and she made this slow hissing sound that would have made a snake tremble.

It kind of scared the heck out of me, to be honest.

But you know who wasn't scared? You know who was madder than ten hornets being woken up from a nap?

Yup, you guessed it.

Abby.

"Let's cancel the meeting for today," I announced quickly, trying to avoid any more nastiness between the two animals.

But judging by the looks in their eyes, I was too late.

It was *game on.*

CHAPTER 5

FACT: Dogs don't like it when you threaten them. But they REALLY don't like it when you threaten their owners.

ABBY'S TWO DIFFERENT-COLORED eyes were boring into Purrkins like lasers, and I suppose it might have been the sun, but they were definitely turning a vampire-ish yellow.

Meanwhile, Purrkins was growling like a ferocious tiger who hadn't hit her growth spurt yet.

"Are they going to attack each other?" Baxter said.

"Don't be ridiculous!" I said, even though I was wondering the exact same thing.

Irwin started fidgeting from one foot to the other, and he rolled the sleeves of his CrimeBiters sweatshirt up and down. "I don't like this," he whimpered. "I don't like this at all."

"Thank you, Captain Obvious," I said, which I know wasn't the nicest thing in the world to say. It was the tension talking, I swear.

Irwin harrumphed, and I turned my attention back to Abby. Her tail was still at full attention, and now it was twitching back and forth, kind of like an antenna in a soft breeze. It definitely wasn't wagging, that's for sure.

I bent down and started petting her back, where she had a long black streak of fur that looked exactly like a cape. "It's okay," I said. "We're all friends here. We're all on the same team."

"That's right," Daisy said, trying to cuddle with Purrkins, even though Purrkins didn't look like she was exactly in a cuddling mood. "Abby is a brave dog who always protects us."

Both animals were very quiet, and after about ten more seconds, Daisy said, "I think we're okay. Things seem to be calmer. I'm going to let Purrkins go." But as soon as Daisy opened her arms to let the cat jump down, Abby started barking at the top of her lungs again. It was a good thing I had put her back on the leash, or else she might have done something stupid. Purrkins, meanwhile, was walking in a circle around Abby, howling, meowing, and giving her the Cat Stare of Death.

Daisy scooped up her pet. "Well, this was definitely a mistake," she hissed, kind of like, well, a cat. "I thought Abby had matured a little bit over the past year, and gotten over her bad behavior. Obviously, I was wrong."

"Wait, what?" I said, feeling the weird tingling in my arms that comes with extreme irritation. "You just said it yourself, Abby protects us! It's your fault for bringing your cat to our meeting without telling anyone." I inserted a short but dramatic pause here. "If Abby is aggressive to Purrkins, it can only mean one thing: your cat is up to no good."

PREVIOUSLY ESTABLISHED FACT: Pets are extremely protective of their owners.

NEW FACT: Owners are even more protective of their pets.

Daisy looked at me with big blue eyes that had suddenly turned as cold as crushed ice. "Fine, have it your way. We're leaving."

And without another word, she turned and walked out the door.

Irwin, Baxter, and I all looked at each other. Then we looked down at Abby, who had decided her work here was done. She stretched, yawned, and promptly lay down for a catnap. I mean a dog nap.

"How can you just fall asleep after that?" I demanded. She didn't respond—maybe because she's a dog—so in my best disciplinarian voice, I added, "And what was that all about anyway? Daisy is our friend!" Hearing Daisy's name, Abby did look up for a second, but after making sure Daisy and her animal were still gone, she went back to her snooze.

"ABBY!" I said, raising my voice. "You can't just sleep! You need to start behaving better—I mean it!"

Irwin's eyes went wide with surprise. "Dude, what is your problem? Leave Abby alone, she's just doing what comes naturally. That's what you love about her, remember?"

"Yeah, Jimmy," Baxter added. "That was a little harsh."

I blinked like I'd just woken up. "It was?" I looked at Abby, who most definitely wasn't sleeping anymore. No, she was looking up at me as if she'd just seen a ghost, and not the friendly kind.

"I'm sorry, Abby," I said. "I'm really sorry I yelled at you."

Abby gave me a wag of forgiveness, which made me feel even worse.

FACT: Dogs don't hold grudges.

I hugged her. "You're still the best dog ever."

"Let's just go," Irwin said. "We've all had enough excitement for one day anyway."

Baxter and I nodded in agreement, and we started walking home. Abby walked much more slowly than usual, like she was still trying to understand what had happened.

"Have you ever yelled at Abby like that before?" Baxter asked me.

"Of course not," I said. "And I feel really bad, you know why? Because it was all that darn cat's fault."

I was pretty sure Irwin rolled his eyes at that one, but I wasn't about to look.

CHAPTER 6

QUESTION: What are the two most horrible, terrible, awful words in the English language?

ANSWER: POP QUIZ.

"POP QUIZ!"

Our math teacher, Ms. Owenby, was smiling when she said it. She was evil that way. She was nice in pretty much every other way, but she really seemed to get a kick out of seeing the shocked, panicky looks on our faces whenever she dropped a bombshell like that.

"NOOOOOOOO!" half the class moaned.

"ON A MONDAY?" hollered the other half.

"Yes," she answered. "Not a big deal. Ten questions. And it will be good preparation for the year-end test coming up in a few weeks."

PROFILE

Name: Ms. Owenby

Age: All teachers seem pretty old, so probably pretty old

Occupation: Math teacher

Interests: Numbers—lots and lots and lots of numbers

Chad Knight raised his hand. "I don't think any of us feel like we need any extra preparation," he said. "We'll study for the test, we promise." The rest of us nodded. Chad was the coolest, most athletic kid in the whole school, and people usually followed his lead. When he quit lacrosse and took up ballroom dancing a few months earlier, two other kids on the team actually did it too. Three weeks later they changed their minds and came back to the team, but Chad stuck with dancing. Now he's Northeast Regional Under-Twelve Champion. Pretty amazing, although my guess is there aren't that many ballroom dancers under twelve in the northeast.

Anyway, however cool and awesome Chad was, Ms. Owenby wasn't buying what he was selling. "I'm sure that's true, Chad," she said. "I'm sure everyone will study for the test. And studying is wonderful, but there's no substitute for the real thing."

You could almost hear the whole class roll their eyes.

I groaned to myself and got a pencil with a good eraser out of my backpack. (With math quizzes, there is always plenty of erasing involved.) I looked around the room, and everyone was doing the same thing, with one exception. Baxter Bratford was sitting across the row from me, sweating buckets. His left leg was jiggling up and down like it was made out of jumping beans, and he was furiously rubbing his legs with his hands.

In other words, he looked completely terrified.

"Are you okay?" I whisper-shouted to him.

"Of course not!" he said. "I don't know any of this stuff! Can you help me?"

"Help you?" I said. "How?"

He looked around the room, and leaned over with a really guilty look on his face. "You know."

I glanced two rows behind me, where Irwin sat. He saw what was going on, and he shrugged sadly. We both felt helpless, but there was nothing we could do.

FACT: I would do almost anything for a fellow CrimeBiter—except let him copy my answers.

"I can't," I told Baxter, and I'm sure I felt even guiltier than he did. "I'm sorry, but I just can't."

He slumped back in his seat. "I know. I'm sorry I asked. That was stupid."

As we started to take the quiz, I kept sneaking glances at Baxter, watching the sweat continue to pour down from his forehead. Then, after about ten minutes, he suddenly raised his hand. "Excuse me? Ms. Owenby? Excuse me? I'm finished."

She looked up. "Really, Baxter? Is everything okay? You can't possibly have finished already."

He violently nodded his head up and down. "I did, Ms. Owenby, I swear. And also, I suddenly feel very sick. I feel like I might throw up. I really need to go to the nurse's office. Really badly. Like right now. Immediately."

Ms. Owenby narrowed her eyes, as if she was trying to decide if Baxter was telling the truth. On the one hand, she knew he was a pretty terrible math student. On the other hand, he did look sicker than ten dogs.

"Okay, fine. Bring me your quiz, and you may be dismissed to go to the nurse's office."

"Thank you, Ms. Owenby." Baxter quickly gathered up all his stuff, shoved it into his backpack, and fled the room. Irwin and I took one last glance at each other and shook our heads.

Our friend was in real trouble.

CHAPTER 7

"YOU KNOW WHAT the crazy thing is, Baxter? The quiz wasn't even hard at all! You could have totally nailed it!"

We were at lunch, and Baxter had returned from his visit to the nurse. Now he was hunched over his tray, contemplating his soggy french fries. He didn't seem sick, but he didn't seem hungry either. "I don't want to talk about it," he moaned. "It will ruin my appetite. Where are the other guys?"

"They're coming." I looked around the cafeteria, desperate for Irwin and Daisy to show up. I waved at Chad, who was having a chocolate-milk–chugging contest with the lacrosse guys. Part of me—okay, most of me—wanted to be over there with them, instead of trying to cheer up Baxter, who seemed determined to be miserable anyway.

We sat there for another minute, eating in silence. Then, out of the blue, Baxter said, "I may have to stay back."

I stopped midchew. "What did you say?"

Baxter sighed heavily and sat back in his chair. "Yup."

Daisy picked that exact moment to skip up to our table in the best mood ever. "Hey, guys! Guess what? I just found out my short story is going to be read out loud at the book fair! How awesome is that?"

Baxter and I looked up at Daisy, and her giant grin immediately vanished. "Whoops," she said. "Bad timing?"

"Yup," I said. "You could say that."

She sat down and started munching on her sandwich. "What's wrong?"

I looked at Baxter. I was pretty sure he didn't want to tell her. I wasn't even sure he wanted to tell me—it might have just slipped out.

But I was wrong. "I'm failing math, and if I don't pass I'm going to have to go to summer school, or maybe even stay back," he told Daisy. She stared at him. "Repeat the grade," he added, as if she didn't get it.

But she got it, all right.

"Well, obviously, that can't happen," she announced. "This is an unacceptable situation that we must correct immediately."

Baxter eyed her gloomily. "Correct how?"

"The same way you correct anything," Daisy said. "Hard work. We will start an after-school study group and get you fully up to speed."

Baxter blinked. "You guys would do that for me?"

"Of course we would!" said Daisy. She looked at me. "Right, Jimmy?"

"Oh yeah, absolutely," I said, although I was already wondering how that was going to work. Figuring out word problems was one thing. Teaching someone else how to do them—especially someone who didn't know how to do them at all—was another thing entirely.

Irwin walked up and fell into his seat with a big groan. "Boy, the line to get pizza was nuts," he said. He shoved a giant bite into his mouth. "What'd I miss?"

FACT: Technically, you're not supposed to talk with your mouth full. But when it comes to pizza, it's kind of hard to resist.

"You missed Daisy and Jimmy being the nicest friends in the world," Baxter said. "I need help with math and you guys are going to help me pass so I don't have to stay back."

Irwin didn't stop chewing. "Help how?"

"After-school tutoring," Daisy said. "We can all chip in."

"There's, like, barely any time left in the school year," Irwin said, his mouth still full. "How are we going to help Baxter get smart in three weeks?"

Baxter looked down, with a wounded look on his face.

"I didn't mean it like that!" Irwin said, even though he kind of did. Back when Baxter was a bully, Irwin always used to talk about how people like Baxter only acted mean because they were insecure about being stupid. And I used to agree with Irwin. I suddenly felt really guilty about that.

"It's not a matter of how, it's a matter of when," Daisy said firmly. "We're friends, and that's what friends do. We'll make sure you pass math, and that's all there is to it." She patted Baxter on the back. "First tutoring session tomorrow after school, at my house."

"How—" Irwin said, but he decided not to finish the sentence. Probably because he knew Daisy wouldn't let him.

"Wow," Baxter said. "Thanks, you guys. Thanks so much!" He turned his attention to his fries and quickly polished them off.

I took that as a sure sign he was feeling better already.

CHAPTER 8

EVERY TIME ABBY and I walk into the Northport ARF, I feel like the luckiest person in the world. Not just because I love working with dogs, but also because I live a nice, safe life, in a nice, safe house, and didn't grow up on the streets scrounging for food in garbage cans.

But every one of the animals at the shelter had lived a scary, unsafe life at some point: so it was my job to make their days as fun and comfortable as possible.

When I got there that afternoon, Shep was busy trying to get a giant bullmastiff to obey his commands.

"Sit, Bruno," Shep said, but the mastiff just stood there sleepily.

Shep tried again. "Sit!" No dice.

Shep sighed, then walked up to Bruno and scratched him behind the ear. The dog groaned with happiness. "I think he probably knows he can take me in a fight," Shep said. "So why should he do anything I say?"

I laughed and started picking up all the discarded toys lying around the training circle, which was always my first responsibility when I got there. "Hey, Shep," I said. "I have a bone to pick with you."

"Dude, nice use of the word *bone*!" he said. "Wassup?"

"Well, I met Daisy's new friend the other day. Her little furry friend."

Shep's eyes were twinkling. "Her little furry, purry friend? Nice! How'd that work out for ya?"

"Not so good, to be honest with you," I told him. "Abby was not very friendly, and Purrkins was no friendlier. Daisy and I ended up getting into a little argument about it."

Shep grinned. "Well, that's gonna happen with cats and dogs, just like with boys and girls. They need a little time to realize they're not enemies. But all will be fine, I promise. Purrkins is a sweetheart, and so is little Abby here."

As if to prove Shep right, Abby went up to big Bruno, gave him a nip on his leg, and started pawing at him playfully. Bruno lazily turned one eye toward Abby and swatted her on the snout. Abby took that as a sign of encouragement, and proceeded to tug on Bruno's ear for thirty seconds. I'm not sure Bruno even noticed.

"See?" I said to Shep. "Dogs belong with dogs."

"Animals belong with animals," Shep said. "Including humans, of course."

"I guess," I mumbled.

Shep took a drink from the giant cup of coffee he always seemed to have in his hand. "You're an apprentice animal trainer, I have faith that you're going to figure it out!" He swallowed, let out a gentle belch, and smacked me on the back. "Welp, gotta go teach some fish how to swim."

"Seriously?"

He grinned. "No."

As I put the toys in the giant bin and watched Abby play with Bruno (I couldn't exactly say that Bruno was playing with Abby, but at least he was tolerating it), I realized something.

If Daisy and I were going to stay best friends, then somehow Abby and Purrkins had to learn how to be best friends too.

CHAPTER 9

MY SISTER, MISTY, likes to watch these ridiculous TV shows where people have contests to see who can make the nicest or coolest dresses and shirts and stuff. It's so boring, if you ask me. But that night after dinner, she was staring with intense fascination as some guy was trying to figure out how to make a pair of pants out of tree bark.

"How can you watch this?" I said.

"You're totally not sophisticated enough to understand," was her answer.

So I decided to do what I often do in this situation.

"MOM! DAD! MISTY'S HOGGING THE TV!"

Misty sneered at me. "What, you want to watch one of those creaky old black-and-white police shows? What are you, an eighty-year-old man trapped in an eleven-year-old's body?"

She was referring to my fondness for a show called

STOP! POLICE!, a crime-fighting show that, it's true, is from about sixty years ago. But so what? Great story-telling never goes out of style.

My parents came into the room, and they both had the same *This is the last thing I need after a long day* expression on their faces.

My mom went first. "Jimmy, do you really have to watch *STOP! POLICE!* again tonight?"

"Can't you just watch it on the computer?" my dad chimed in.

"No!" I said. "It's so much better on the big screen! And besides, there's a marathon on tonight! They're showing all seventy-eight episodes in a row!"

My parents looked at each other and sighed.

FACT: Parents looking at each other and sighing = lecture coming.

"Jimmy," said my dad. "Mom and I both love how passionate you are about some things. It's part of what makes you so special."

FACT: Parents telling you you're special = never a good sign.

My mom jumped in. "The thing is though, it's not great when a passion becomes an obsession."

I didn't take my eyes off the TV, even though the guy who made the tree pants was now making a hat out of leaves. "I don't know what that means," I said. "I just like one show. What's so bad about that?"

"Nothing!" said my dad. "But . . . when you combine it with your gang, and doing all these training exercises, and, well, you know, thinking that Abby has special crime-fighting capabilities—"

"I don't *think*, I *know*," I corrected him.

"You're busy," my dad said. "With schoolwork, and lacrosse, and after school at the shelter. It's a lot. We just don't want you to be spread too thin, that's all."

"Are you asking me to give up the CrimeBiters?" I asked, in a *not happening* kind of way.

"Of course not," my mom said. "But maybe you guys could take a break for a few weeks? Just until the school year ends?"

"Forget it."

My dad sat down on the arm of the couch. "You sure? You can pick it back up just as soon as summer comes."

I decided to change strategy. "Just so you guys know, my friends and I do a lot more than just CrimeBiters stuff.

45

Like tomorrow after school, we're tutoring Baxter because he's failing math, and we have to help him pass the last test or else he might get left back."

"Oh, poor Baxter," said my mom. My strategy worked—she wasn't talking about the CrimeBiters anymore.

Misty groaned. "Can you guys stop talking? This is, like, the part where they decide who's Fashion Forward!"

We all stared at Misty, who was glued to this absurd TV show. Then I looked at my parents.

"And you say *I'm* obsessed?"

CHAPTER 10

THE NEXT DAY, I could tell right when I walked into math class that something was wrong. It wasn't just that Ms. Owenby, who is almost always in a good mood (math makes her happy—go figure), was standing there with a grim expression.

It was that Mr. Klondike was standing right next to her.

FACT: The six scariest words in the English language are "Please go to Mr. Klondike's office."

Mr. Klondike is our vice-principal. That means he's the adult in charge of punishment. If you do anything wrong, and I do mean *anything*, you will find yourself staring up at him in his super scary office, stammering out some sort of excuse.

PROFILE

Name: Mr. Klondike

Age: I don't know, and I don't want to know

Occupation: Vice-principal

Interests: Scaring the daylights out of defenseless little children

I guess what I'm trying to say is, Mr. Klondike is not the guy you want to see standing at the front of the classroom when you walk into math. His son Kermit is in our class, and even *he* scares the daylights out of me. Baxter used to be friends with him, back in Baxter's mean bully days. That's kind of all you really need to know about Kermit Klondike.

We all quietly took our seats and waited. And waited, and waited some more. It seemed like Mr. Klondike just wanted to make us sweat for a few minutes before telling us why he was there. And it worked.

"Class," said Ms. Owenby, finally. "We have had a very disappointing development over the last twenty-four hours. Very disappointing, indeed. I will turn it over to Mr. Klondike to explain."

Mr. Klondike took his glasses off, cleaned them with his tie, put them back on, stroked his chin, took a sip of water, cleared his throat, and stared at us for a full minute. The guy could really terrify a room full of kids, that's for sure.

"We have had a breach," he said. None of us knew what a *breach* was, but we were all pretty sure it wasn't good. "A terrible breach of trust has been perpetrated upon this community." *Yes!* I knew what *perpetrated* meant. I couldn't wait to tell my parents that watching *STOP! POLICE!* had improved my vocabulary . . .

But hold on a second. This was no time to be happy about anything. The hammer was about to fall.

"Ms. Owenby has informed me that the answer sheet for her quiz from yesterday is missing. It was in her bottom desk drawer, and now it's gone." Mr. Klondike narrowed his eyes, exactly the way Hank Barlow (the hero of *STOP! POLICE!*) does when he's about to arrest a criminal. "Her concern is that someone took it before she administered the quiz, in order to get all the answers right."

The whole class let out a silent gasp. Was Mr. Klondike saying what we thought he was saying? Was he actually suggesting that someone in the class *stole* the answer sheet?

"That would be cheating, children," he said, eliminating all doubt. "And it is perhaps the most serious offense a student can commit in school."

Holy smokes.

"This is an unfortunate situation," Ms. Owenby said. "Very unfortunate. But that doesn't mean it can't be

corrected. Mr. Klondike has been gracious enough to offer the following: if whoever took the answer sheet goes quietly to his office at any point today and admits this terrible mistake, it will be resolved without punishment."

Mr. Klondike looked around the room as if trying to figure out right then and there who did it. "But if that doesn't happen, and the student is later caught, there will be real consequences," he said, with a scary gleam in his eye. "The perpetrator will be in serious trouble, and the punishment may include suspension, or even possible expulsion."

This time you could hear the gasp from the kids, loud and clear. Mr. Klondike nodded slowly to no one in particular, then walked out of the classroom without another word. Ms. Owenby walked to the blackboard and picked up a piece of chalk, getting ready to start the lesson. "Well. Let's put that behind us for now. I very much hope it is resolved quickly, so we can all move on." She started to write a math problem on the board. "Who's ready to get back to work?"

Unlike most of Ms. Owenby's questions, that was an easy one.

The answer was no one.

CHAPTER 11

AT LUNCH, BAXTER, Daisy, Irwin, and I all sat down at our usual table and started eating. No one said a word. I think we were all still trying to absorb the news that someone in our grade was a thief and a cheater.

The only person who was in a good mood was Daisy, who wasn't in our math class. "Cheer up, you guys!" she said. "It's not like one of you guys did it!"

"Of course not," I said. "It's just the fact that someone would be so crazy is kind of hard to believe."

"Some people don't know any better," Daisy said. "Some people get scared, or they panic, and then the next thing you know they're doing something they would never ordinarily do."

"And once it's done, there's no taking it back," I added. "You're kind of stuck."

"At least Mr. Klondike said he wouldn't punish the

kid if he turned himself in," Irwin said. "That's pretty nice of him. I didn't realize he was actually capable of being nice."

"Neither did I," I said.

Daisy popped a cracker into her mouth. "Well, all I know is, I feel sorry for the person who did it," she said. "They probably wish they'd never done it, and now the choice is to either pray you don't get caught, or go down to the scariest room ever invented—Mr. Klondike's office."

"The poor kid," Irwin and I said at the same time. Then he said, "I sure wouldn't want to be him right now."

"I wish I knew who it was," I added. "I'd tell them to go to Mr. Klondike's office for sure."

"Absolutely!" Daisy said.

Irwin chomped on his eggplant sandwich (he had very weird taste in food). "You have to be pretty desperate to do something like that," he said. "I mean, who would risk getting thrown out of school just to pass one stinking quiz?"

"The only possible reason for doing something like that is if you were in danger of flunking the whole class," I said. "That's how desperate you'd have to be."

Irwin looked at me. I looked at him. We both looked at Daisy.

Then all three of us looked at Baxter.

I think we all realized at the same time that he hadn't said anything the whole time we'd been sitting there. Not to mention the fact that Baxter *was* in danger of flunking the whole class. And just might be desperate and crazy enough to do something like this.

Baxter, who was sitting there with one hand on his chin and the other hand trying to stab a noodle with his fork, looked up and saw the three of us staring at him.

"What?"

We all sat there, none of us sure what to say. Finally, Daisy said, "You're being so quiet."

"Well, I don't really have a whole lot to say," Baxter mumbled. "You guys seem to have it all covered anyway."

"Who do you think stole the answer sheet?" Irwin asked. "Like, do you have any guesses or anything?"

"No, I don't have any guesses." It was clear Baxter didn't want to talk about it. In fact, he didn't really want to talk about anything related to math, if he could help it. But there was just something a little off about the whole thing, and before I knew it, I blurted out the question on everyone's mind.

"You definitely didn't have anything to do with it, right, Bax?"

I thought maybe if I used his nickname—Bax— that he would take the question in the friendly, non-accusatory manner in which it was intended.

He didn't.

"Are you kidding me right now?" he said, raising his voice. "Are you kidding me? Do you actually think I would do something so stupid, not to mention illegal?"

"Of course not," I stammered.

"No way," Irwin added.

"That's crazy," Daisy joined in.

"Although you did finish the quiz really fast," Irwin added, because he couldn't help himself.

Baxter stood up so fast he almost knocked his chair over. "You know something? You guys have never really trusted me. I can tell. You still think I'm the dumb, mean bully I was when you first met me. That's who I'll always be to you, no matter what." He picked up his tray. "Well, not anymore. I'm done with all this. And no—I DIDN'T TAKE THE FREAKIN' ANSWER SHEET. I FINISHED

THE QUIZ FAST BECAUSE I DIDN'T KNOW ANY OF THE ANSWERS. HAPPY NOW?"

He said the last few sentences so loud that every head in the place turned in our direction. I saw Mr. Klondike's son Kermit, who was three tables over, elbow one of his bully buddies in the ribs and say, "Losers."

As Baxter stormed away, Daisy, Irwin, and I sat there in silence. After a few seconds, Daisy sighed.

"Well, there's only one way to get Baxter to forgive us for thinking he might have stolen the answers," she said.

I looked at her. "What's that?"

Daisy flashed her determined Daisy face.

"Find out who did."

AFTER MY AFTER-SCHOOL snack, I put Abby on the leash and we went across the street to Daisy's house, to help Baxter with his math. Daisy and Irwin were already there, and we were all wearing our CrimeBiters sweatshirts. We were all set to go, except there was one thing missing: Baxter.

We were all pretty certain he wasn't going to show up: I think he'd rather fail that test and stay back than face the so-called friends who had betrayed him.

"The answer-sheet mystery is definitely a solvable case," I said, even though I had no idea how to solve it. We were sitting in Daisy's backyard, with Abby snoozing under a tree. Daisy had suggested we all stay outside, so Abby and Purrkins wouldn't have to run into each other. I agreed, although I remembered my conversation with Shep, and I was still determined to make Abby and Purrkins friends. How hard could it be?

FACT: Trying to get a cat and a dog to be friends is very, very hard.

"I agree," Daisy said. "It's totally solvable. We just need to do a little detective work."

"That's our specialty," I agreed.

"I have an idea!" Irwin said. "Tomorrow, at recess, we can start a conversation about it. Like we're trying to figure out who the thief is. Then we look around and see if anyone is listening to us, and acting nervous or suspicious in some way."

I was skeptical. "Wait, so you think someone is just going to hear us talking about it and say, 'Oh, I'm the person you're looking for?'"

"No, silly," said Daisy. "They would never admit it. But they might do something that indicates guilt."

Irwin snickered at me. "Don't you know that from all the police shows you watch?" I immediately felt embarrassed, because he was right—I should have known.

"I have another idea," I said, trying to save face. "What if one of us pretends to admit it, and then we all look around to see who seems to be in a particularly good mood, and we'll know that that's the person that did it, because they're so happy that someone else is confessing?"

"That's a terrible idea," Irwin said.

"No it's not!" I said back.

We both looked at Daisy.

"It *is* pretty terrible," she said.

"Fine," I said, "we'll try Irwin's idea, but it better work. We just need to figure out what Abby should do."

"What does Abby have to do with it?" Irwin asked. "We're doing our detective work at school. Last I checked, dogs don't go to school."

"Ha-ha-ha," I said, trying to think. "But later on, we might end up at the person's house when we try to catch them. We'll need Abby then."

Irwin snorted. "That's a stretch, but whatever."

"Purrkins can come too," I added.

Daisy scrunched up her nose. "Purrkins? Why?"

"We may need extra help with this one."

Judging by the expressions on Daisy's and Irwin's faces, that was my second terrible idea in the last two minutes. I was on a roll.

"Okay, fine, maybe that's dumb," I admitted. "I just want them to be friends, is that so bad? Shep said they just need to spend a little time together and they'll be fine."

"You want me to go get Purrkins?" Daisy asked. "Try it now?"

"Or we can bring Abby into your house," I said. "Whichever's better."

"I prefer to not watch this," offered Irwin.

"I'll be right back," Daisy said. She went to get the cat, leaving Irwin and me sitting there on her back porch.

Irwin sat there for a second, fidgeting around, before saying, "Are we absolutely, positively, one hundred percent sure that Baxter didn't steal that answer sheet?"

I stared at him. "Are you serious right now? He barely even *took* the quiz!"

"I'm just saying!" Irwin's eyes darted back and forth. "Maybe he stole it but then, like, lost it or something. We can't be sure."

"I'm sure," I said. "Baxter was super insulted that we even thought that for a second. And I don't blame him."

"Okay," mumbled Irwin, but he didn't seem totally convinced.

"Here we are!" sang Daisy, as she came outside. Just like the day before, she was holding Purrkins in her hand, but this time, the cat didn't look nervous at all. This time, she looked tough—like, *You're in my house now.*

Abby took one look at her and scampered under my chair.

"Abby?" I said. "Whatcha doing down there?" I peered down and saw her shaking like a leaf.

Whoa.

FACT: Trembling with fear is bad for a crime-fighting vampire dog's reputation.

"Ha-ha-ha-ha-ha-ha!" Irwin crowed. "She's totally scared of Purrkins!" Then, as if I hadn't heard him the first time, he added, "Ha-ha-ha-ha-ha-ha-ha-ha!"

"I've—I've never seen her do that before," I stammered. "She's never afraid of anything."

"Scaredy-dog! Scaredy-dog!" Irwin sang, before I silenced him with a glare.

Daisy bent down. "Come on out of there, Abby," she said gently. "Purrkins isn't going to do anything." She scratched Purrkins's belly, and the cat gave out a long, contented purr. "She's a love bug, aren't you, Purrky Purrky Purr?"

I could have done without the nickname, but I appreciated Daisy's effort. Unfortunately though, Abby seemed frozen in place.

"Maybe I'll put her down, and see how that goes," Daisy suggested.

"That's a good idea," Irwin said. "Otherwise Abby might be stuck under there all night."

"Jimmy, okay by you?"

I nodded. Who was I to disagree with Daisy Flowers?

FACT: Every once in a while—like, once every four million times—Daisy Flowers is wrong.

Daisy put Purrkins down, and the next thing I knew, Abby ran to the corner of the patio and started howling her head off. But it was worse than at the Boathouse, because this time, Purrkins was howling back, and the two of them were circling each other like two heavyweights getting ready to fight for the world championship.

The only good news was that by some miracle, neither one of them made the first move.

"ABBY!" I yelled, freaking out.

"PURRKINS!" Daisy yelled, also freaking out.

"WHAT DID I TELL YOU?" Irwin hollered, enjoying every second of it.

Daisy quickly scooped up Purrkins and ran back inside. Abby stopped barking, panted for a minute, went over to the water bowl and drank about three gallons of water, and then lay down and stared at the sliding door, waiting for the threat to return.

Daisy came back out and plopped down in the chair next to me.

"Okay, maybe no pets on this case," she said.

"Why no pets at all?" I said. "Abby is a CrimeBiter. Purrkins isn't. Abby should still be able to be part of the mission."

Daisy sighed. "Are we actually arguing about this? Jeez, Jimmy, sometimes no one can be right but you. Fine. Whatever you say."

I stared at her. Was she actually going to let a cat ruin our friendship?

FACT: Shep was right. People were crazy when it came to their pets. And yes: I include myself in that category.

"Fine yourself," I said, refusing to look at her. "Have it your way. No pets."

Irwin threw up his hands in relief.

"Now we're getting somewhere," he said.

CHAPTER 13

ON THE WALK home from Daisy's house, I said to Abby, "So let me get this straight—you have no problem taking on a dangerous diamond thief and a crazy lacrosse coach, but one little kitty cat sends you diving under a chair?"

Abby looked a little embarrassed, to tell you the truth. But that was all I got out of her.

"I know it might seem hard to believe right now," I went on, "but Daisy and I may very well get married one day, so you're going to have to learn to get along with Purrkins at some point." Then I added, "The marriage thing is just between us, by the way."

Back home, Mrs. Cragg, my babysitter, was making her famous cinnamon apple muffins. They smelled amazing. It was hard to believe, but when I first met Mrs. Cragg, she was my archenemy. She hated Abby; helped her brother, Barnaby Bratford, steal my mom's necklace; and—maybe worst of all—fed me seaweed for dinner. Now, she was one of my favorite adults—besides my parents, of course. And Shep. And Isaac, the baking genius who makes the farmer's market a worthwhile place to visit, despite all the zucchinis they sell.

"Jimmy!" she cried. "Just in time, I'm about to take them out of the oven."

"Are Dad or Misty home?"

She shook her head. "No, sir. Misty is at Jarrod's baseball game, and your dad is working today." It was always good news when my dad was working, even though I liked having him around the house.

"Got it. Can you take me to the shelter?"

"That's what I'm here for!"

As I ate one of her yummy muffins, I explained to Mrs. Cragg what had happened that day: about the test, and falsely accusing Baxter, and the difficulty Daisy and I were having getting our pets to become friends.

"Sounds like a trying day," said Mrs. Cragg. "But I happen to know that your friendships are strong enough to withstand a few bumps in the road. And in the meantime, you have the shelter, where you can go to forget about all that stuff."

I nodded. Mrs. Cragg was right: the shelter was the one place I could get away from it all.

FACT: Nothing can cheer a guy up more than a bunch of dogs who are happy to see you.

On the way there, I fell asleep in the car, and dreamed that Abby and Purrkins were best friends, and they were playing in my backyard, and Daisy and I were sitting there watching them and laughing.

It was the best dream ever.

Then I woke up.

CHAPTER 14

THE FIRST THING I noticed when I walked into the shelter was that Shep wasn't his usual happy, whistling self. Instead, he was on the phone, pacing around with his head down, waving his free arm around like he was swatting flies. I was about to go up to him to see if there was anything I could do, but when he saw me coming he waved me away, whispering, "Not now, Jimmy. Not now."

So I took Abby and headed to the outdoor training ring, where I saw Kelsey, Shep's head trainer, teaching a King Charles spaniel several commands.

"Weave," Kelsey said to the spaniel. "Wait. Follow your star."

I smiled. It wasn't that long ago that Shep was out here with Abby, training her to stop destroying my mom's shoes and act like a seminormal dog. It ended up working a little too well.

PROFILE

Name: Kelsey Breed

Age: Not sure, but I do know she's from London, England

Occupation: Animal trainer (probably because of her last name)

Interests: Using weird words that I don't understand

FACT: The scary story of how Abby almost became like a normal dog is told in the previous CrimeBiters book. Spoiler alert: she didn't lose her powers!

I waved, and Kelsey came over with the spaniel. Since it was a dog and not a cat, Abby was happy to say hi by doing, you know, the usual stuff. (You know what I'm talking about, right? Is it okay if I don't go into details? Great.)

"This dog has me knackered," Kelsey said. Like I said, she used a lot of words that sounded like a foreign language, even though they were in English.

"What's going on?" I asked Kelsey. "Shep looks like he's on an intense phone call."

"I haven't a clue," Kelsey said, "but it's not good. Hey, Jimmy, would you be a lovely chap and pick up the extra bacon wraps?" She was referring to the bacon that Shep strapped to a chair, which was part of the training process.

FACT: If you can get a dog to ignore bacon, you can get a dog to do anything.

A few minutes later, Shep hung up the phone. He had a grim expression on his face as he told the people who worked there to gather around.

"Hey, everyone," Shep said. "Well, yeah, I got some news. After a few false alarms, the day that we knew might come is finally here. It's just been confirmed that our building has been sold, to some developer who is planning on turning this whole block into a shopping center. Unfortunately, that means we're going to have to close the shelter at the end of next month."

No way.

People gasped in shock, and started shouting things like "No!" and "We won't go!" Shep shushed them with his hand. "It is what it is. The rent has been going up for years anyway, so it was only a matter of time. We will look for another place, but we may not find something for a while."

"What will happen to the animals?" someone shouted.

"Who bought the building?" yelled someone else.

Then someone swore, and then someone else swore, and suddenly it was a cursefest in there.

FACT: It's wrong to swear. Unless someone tells you the animal shelter you work at is going to close. Then it's still wrong to swear, but at least it's understandable.

"Please," Shep said. "Please. Yelling and screaming isn't going to do any good. And as for who bought it, it's one of those private real estate investment companies, and apparently their lawyer doesn't have to say who the actual investors are. I guess they've chosen to remain anonymous. And for good reason, since I know a lot of you would like to tell them a choice word or two." People laughed, but it was an angry laugh. "Let's just give our animals the most love we can until the day we close our doors for good. It's the least we can do for those in our care, who depend on us. Thank you."

Everyone went up to Shep to either console him or beg him to fight back. But I could tell by the look in his eyes that he wasn't going to do that. He looked like he just wanted to go home.

"This is bloody awful," said Kelsey. I wasn't sure what blood had to do with it, but I knew what she meant.

Finally, Shep spotted me out of the corner of his eye and came over. The first thing he did was bend down and pet Abby, who licked his hand and leaned into his legs. I think Abby knew what was going on and was trying to make Shep feel better.

Shep smiled. "It's dogs like this girl right here that will make me miss this most of all."

"I don't get it," I said. "Who would kick a bunch of animals out of the only home they've ever had?"

"People who are desperate for another nail salon, or another bank, or another overpriced coffee shop, that's who."

"Well, I'm going to find out who those people are, and I'm going to talk them out of it."

Shep shook his head sadly. "I wish it were that easy. These people with the money, they've got a lot of lawyers and accountants and people in fancy clothes that they can hide behind. And there's no law that says they have to tell you exactly who they are. Believe me, I've tried." He stuck his hand out. "I've loved having you help out, Jimmy. I hope you keep working with animals, no matter what happens. Deal?"

I shook his hand. "Deal."

Shep walked off to talk with some other people, leaving me and Abby standing there. I suddenly felt a little overwhelmed about everything that was happening. I had a case to solve at school, a friend who was about to fail math, another friend who I was fighting with because our pets hated each other, and my favorite place in the world was about to be turned into a shopping mall.

I hate to admit it, but I was about to start crying.

FACT: Boys cry sometimes, and they shouldn't be ashamed to admit it. Although I never cry. Honest! It's true! I swear!

The next thing I knew, Bruno, the giant but lazy mastiff, came running over to Abby. It turned out he wasn't lazy after all; instead, he and Abby started tearing around the training circle, nipping and yowling and chasing each other.

Watching them, I stopped almost-crying.

Then I smiled.

Then I laughed for about ten minutes straight.

VERY IMPORTANT FACT: Watching dogs play is pretty much the best cure for sadness ever invented.

It felt so good to feel better.

If only for a little while.

PART TWO

THE WRONG MAN

CHAPTER 15

WHO DOESN'T LOVE recess?

Well, a long time ago, me.

And by a long time ago, I mean last year.

Back then, it was just me and Irwin, trying to fend off Baxter and his bully friends. So yeah, I wasn't a huge fan. But now, it's a totally different story. Sometimes, I'll hang around with Irwin, Daisy, and (the new and improved) Baxter, sitting on the swings and discussing the latest bad movie or fun video game or good TV show. Sometimes, I'll hang around with Chad Knight and the sports kids, punching each other in the arm and talking about nothing (middle school boys are good at both of those activities).

But today, we had real business to attend to.

CrimeBiters business.

"Where is the best place to do this?" whispered Irwin,

referring to our plan to expose the quiz thief. Irwin always got a little nervous when we were on a case.

"Somewhere that's crowded," Daisy said. "And stop whispering."

"Stop telling him what to do," I told Daisy.

"*You* stop telling *me* what to do," she told me back.

Irwin grinned, which was his usual reaction when Daisy and I bickered with each other.

"I don't know about this," Baxter said uneasily. We were glad he'd joined us, since he hadn't shown up for after-school tutoring and we weren't sure if he'd ever speak to us again. But apparently a good night's sleep had softened his heart. That was the good news. The bad news was, he wasn't exactly a huge fan of our idea.

A bunch of kids were hanging around the playground, so that looked like the perfect spot to put the plan into action.

"You start," said Irwin to me, still whispering.

"Why?" I said. "It was your idea."

Daisy rolled her eyes. "Are you two serious? Sheesh, it's a miracle we ever solve anything."

"I wish Abby was here," I mumbled. This was the first

mission we'd ever been on without her, and it didn't feel right.

Daisy chuckled. "Like, I'm sure the school would just let you take your dog to recess."

"Whatever," I said. "So go ahead and start already."

Daisy cleared her throat. "HEY," she said, really loudly, "THAT ANSWER SHEET THING IS CRAZY. DO YOU GUYS HAVE ANY IDEA WHO MIGHT HAVE DONE IT?"

"I THINK I KNOW," I said, also loudly. "IN FACT, I'M PRETTY SURE I ACTUALLY SAW HIM DO IT."

"YOU DID?" Irwin said, shouting ridiculously loud. "WHO?"

"Irwin, stop shouting like a maniac," Daisy said.

"SORRY!" Irwin shouted, like a maniac.

"YEAH, WHO WAS IT?" Daisy asked.

"I DON'T WANT TO TELL ON HIM," I said. "THAT WOULD BE MEAN."

And just like that, we had our first bite. Kermit Klondike, who was listening to our conversation with his friends, wandered over with his usual annoying swagger.

"What are you guys talking about?" Kermit asked.

PROFILE

Name: Kermit Klondike

Age: Old enough to have a light mustache

Occupation: The vice-principal's son

Interests: Acting tough because he knows he'll never get in trouble

"Oh, nothing," Daisy said, which was our planned answer.

Kermit snorted. "Liar! You guys were talking about the stolen answer sheet. I heard you!"

"I don't know what you're talking about," I said.

Kermit looked at Baxter and shook his head. "I can't believe you're actually friends with these clowns," he said, sneering. Then he turned his attention back to me. "I heard you say you know who took it. 'I saw him,' you said."

By now, Kermit's pals had wandered over to listen. I was either pretending to be nervous or was nervous, I'm not quite sure which. "Maybe."

"Well, how do you know it was a he?" Kermit demanded. "If you didn't see him, how do you know it was a he?"

"What does that even mean?" Irwin asked.

"It means Bishop is lying! Aren't you, Bishop? Admit it. You didn't see anything!"

"Yeah!" said one of Kermit's friends, a wannabe bully named Carl.

"I don't want to talk about this anymore," I said. "Leave me alone."

Kermit gave me one last glare. "You're so lucky the teachers are watching us right now. But as soon as they turn their backs, I'm coming for you." He jabbed a finger in my direction. "You don't want to be making stuff up about people. That can get you in real trouble, if you know what I mean."

He leaned in close enough that I could smell the tuna fish he'd had for lunch. *Eeeeew.* "See you later, dorks."

Kermit walked away with his friends, leaving the four of us standing there.

"Jeez, Baxter, I can't believe you were ever friends with that guy," Irwin said, saying what we were all thinking.

"It was a long time ago," Baxter said.

"Not that long," I said.

Baxter looked embarrassed. "Well, sor-ry."

Irwin shushed us. "All I know," he said, "is that for someone who's that scary and mean, there's only one thing that can happen."

We all looked at him.

"He'll grow up to be vice-principal some day."

CHAPTER 16

"HELLO? HELLO?"

I walked in the door after school, but nobody was home.

Not Dad, not Misty, not Mrs. Cragg.

Not even Abby.

"Where is everybody?"

FACT: People always shout "Where is everybody?" when nobody is around to answer the question.

I wandered into the kitchen and made myself a bowl of cereal, and then I went into the family room, plopped down on the couch, turned on the TV, and immediately fell asleep.

I woke up with a dog sitting on my lap, licking my face and whacking her tail against my knees.

"Abby, off," I said grumpily. "Off!"

Misty came in and immediately started laughing. "Mrs. Cragg and I took Abby for a walk," she said. "And guess what? On our way home we ran into Daisy and her new cat, Purrkins! She's so cute!"

Mrs. Cragg came into the room, nodding. "I have to agree," she said, turning the TV off (my parents had a strict no-TV-during-the-day policy). "Now generally, I'm a dog person, but that was one adorable kitty cat."

I sat up and rubbed my eyes. "But what about Abby?" I asked them. "Didn't Abby and Purrkins start fighting? Did you guys have to run all the way back here?"

Misty and Mrs. Cragg looked at each other like I was crazy. "They seemed like friends to me," Misty said.

"I didn't notice anything either," agreed Mrs. Cragg.

Now I was wide awake. "That's not possible," I said. "They hate each other."

"They got along just fine today," Mrs. Cragg said.

Now I was wide awake and mad. "Why won't Abby be nice to Purrkins when I'm there? And why does Daisy make me feel bad about it? It's not fair."

Mrs. Cragg laughed. "You know, Jimmy, pets feed off their owners quite a bit. If Abby and Purrkins sense tension between you and Daisy when you get together, well then, it's likely that they'll have a bit of tension between themselves as well."

"But they started it!" I protested. "Daisy and I only started fighting after Purrkins and Abby started fighting!"

Mrs. Cragg shrugged. "Sounds like everyone needs to be doing a bit of making up."

As Misty and Mrs. Cragg went back into the kitchen to fix a snack, I looked at Abby, who was still sitting on top of me.

"Is that true?" I asked her. "Well, I promise to make up with Daisy today, okay? Deal?"

But Abby didn't answer.

Maybe because she's a dog.

CHAPTER 17

SINCE WE ROTATED houses for our after-school activities, I had to get a ride over to Irwin's house for the study group. Mrs. Cragg drove me, which was fine, although it meant having to listen to that goofy radio station where the lady gives people advice about their boyfriends and girlfriends the whole time.

"How can you listen to this?" I asked.

"How can I not?" she answered, which made no sense, but I wasn't about to argue.

"You seem a little down, Jimmy," Mrs. Cragg said. "Everything okay?"

"Sure," I said. Then I paused, trying to decide how honest I should be. "I'm a little mad at Abby and Daisy, I guess."

"Well, I completely understand," she said. "But I have a feeling everything will work out. Just when things seem at their worst, something happens that will restore your spirits. Life is funny that way." Mrs. Cragg turned into Irwin's driveway. "Have fun. Call me when you're ready to be picked up."

"I will. Thanks, Mrs. Cragg."

She smiled, and it seemed so hard to believe that way back when, we started out as enemies. If I could become friends with Mrs. Cragg, I could definitely make up with Daisy!

When I walked into Irwin's house, Baxter was already sitting at the kitchen table, working on a math problem. Irwin was on one side of him, and Daisy on the other. Irwin waved. Daisy didn't.

"Hello, Jimmy!" chirped Irwin's mom. "Would you like a glass of juice?" She was a bit of a health nut, so I had no idea what would be in that juice, but I was really thirsty.

"That would be great, Mrs. Wonk, thanks."

She handed me a greenish-orange liquid, and I took a sip. Not bad. Not good, but not bad.

I went over to the guys. Baxter was scratching his head. "This stuff is so HARD!"

"You're getting the hang of it, you really are," Daisy said. Then she looked up at me. "Oh, hello."

Oh, hello?

FACT: Saying "Oh, hello" to someone is like saying "You smell bad."

"*Oh, hello* to you too," I said.

Irwin giggled.

"I don't want to work on math anymore," Baxter said. "Can we go outside and jump on the trampoline?" Irwin had this amazing trampoline that he barely ever used, because he said it sometimes made him seasick. What a waste.

"Not yet!" Daisy said. "You need to study! Do you want someone like Kermit Klondike passing this test and you failing it?"

"That can't happen," agreed Irwin. "That kid is such a jerk."

"And he was acting even jerkier than usual today," Daisy added.

"Maybe he did it," I blurted out, before realizing it.

Baxter, Irwin, and Daisy all turned to me.

"Maybe who did what?" Baxter asked.

"Maybe Kermit stole the answer sheet," I answered.

"Are you crazy?" Daisy said. "His dad's the vice-principal."

"So what?" My heart started racing as I realized I might have just solved the case. "That actually makes him more likely to do it, because he would think he could totally get away with it."

Daisy still looked skeptical, but Irwin nodded. "Hmmmmm. It's true that that was our plan all along," he said. "To talk about the quiz at recess and see who reacted oddly? Well, Kermit sure did."

"There's something else," I said. "His first and last names both start with the same letter."

Everyone looked at me, confused.

"Just like Barnaby Bratford," I added.

We all stood there awkwardly. Barnaby was Baxter's dad, the jewelry thief we'd caught in our first case, before Bax became our friend.

"That's not a very nice thing to bring up," Daisy said.

"Sorry," I said.

Baxter didn't seem to mind though. "It's okay. Just help me pass this test, and you can say whatever you want."

"So we have a suspect," I said. "We will pursue this tomorrow at school. Are we all agreed?"

Everyone looked at Daisy. It was clear that she had to say yes before anyone else dared to.

"We're agreed," she said. "Thank you, Jimmy, for your expert analysis of this case."

I smiled. I'd made a breakthrough on the case, and Daisy was being nice to me again!

Mrs. Cragg was right.

Life *is* funny that way.

CHAPTER 18

AFTER BAXTER ANSWERED three straight problems correctly, we decided that was enough math for one day, and we went outside and jumped on the trampoline for a half hour.

FACT: Trampoline is a lot more fun than math.

Finally, Mrs. Wonk came outside. "Jimmy? Your dad is here." Then she offered me a brownie that had what looked like pencil shavings on top.

"Gluten-free carob sprinkles," she explained.

"No thanks," I said. And also, *eeeewwww.*

FACT: When you have a brownie, there's no need to mess it up with other stuff.

I went out to the driveway and saw my dad sitting in the car, with Abby in the backseat. I felt both happy and worried, which is what happens whenever I see my dad during the day. Happy, because he's home. Worried, because that might mean his job fell through. That's what happens when you have a dad who has been working on and off for a while.

"Dad? Is everything okay?"

He grinned. "Everything's great! Hop in!" As I climbed in the passenger seat, he added, "Had a meeting nearby and decided to play hooky for the rest of the day. I'll drop you at the shelter."

My heart soared with relief. "Awesome!"

I turned around to say hi to Abby. She gave me a big wag and a slurpy lick on my nose. "Yuck!" I groaned, but it was a happy groan.

"Everything go okay in there?" my dad asked.

"Yup. We did some work with Baxter on his math, and then we jumped on the trampoline." I almost told him about Kermit and the stolen answer sheet, but for some reason I just decided not to. I think because I knew he would have asked a million questions and I didn't really feel like giving a million answers.

When we got to the shelter, I noticed that it looked

totally different already. There were a bunch of boxes all over the place, with labels like TOYS and BONES and COLLARS and FOOD.

"What's going on?" my dad said. As we walked over to Shep and Kelsey, who were loading up boxes, I realized I hadn't told my parents about the shelter. Maybe because I didn't want to believe it myself.

"The shelter has to close, Dad," I said. "Someone bought it and is turning it into a shopping center."

"Oh no! That totally stinks."

"Yup," Shep grunted, huffing and puffing as he and

Kelsey lifted a giant dog bed into a box that said RANDOM STUFF. "Getting ready for the big sale."

"What big sale?"

"The big blowout everything-must-go sale!" Shep sighed. "Thank God for eBay."

"I'm gutted over this whole thing," Kelsey said to me. "Simply gutted."

"Me too," I said, even though I had no idea what she was talking about.

FACT: English English is a totally different language than American English.

My dad grabbed a side of the bed and helped them stuff it into the box. As soon as they were done, Abby proceeded to jump into the box and lie down in the bed.

"Abby likes small, dark places," I said.

"And I don't think she wants you to go," my dad added.

Shep laughed sadly.

Dad reached into the box and pulled Abby out. "I'm really sorry to hear about your shelter, Shep," he said. "This is a terrific place. I can still remember coming here last year and picking up this crazy little dog. She sneezed all over me!"

"I remember that," Shep said, smiling.

"Me too," I said. "And Dad, remember when we were filling out the paperwork, you asked me what I wanted to name her, and I said Happy, but you heard me wrong and wrote down Abby?"

"I sure do." Dad put Abby on the floor and turned to Shep. "I don't suppose there's anything we can do to help?"

"Not unless you got a couple of million dollars lying around," Shep said.

"Let me check the car," my dad said, and for a split second I actually thought he was serious.

FACT: Hope can make you really gullible sometimes.

"Jimmy," Shep said, "you've been a great help to me these last few months. I really appreciate it. But I'm going to wrap up all training classes this week, and I need to start finding other shelters for the animals." He bent down to my level so he could look me in the eye. "And frankly, buddy, I don't think you want to be around here, getting sadder and sadder. That won't be much fun for either of us."

My lower lip started to tremble. "Uh . . . are you firing me?"

"Of course not! You're my guy!" Shep gave me a big

bear hug. "But we should probably start to wind things down, okay? How about you help me out one more week, and then we'll call it a day, okay? As soon as I figure out my next move, you'll be right there with me."

"How are you going to be able to find homes for all the animals?" I asked Shep.

"Not sure," he said, "but I'll figure something out."

I looked up at my dad. "We have to do something! I need to help Shep save his shelter!"

"Really?" My dad raised his eyebrows. "How are you going to do that?"

"I don't know yet," I said. "But I am."

He gave my shoulder a little squeeze. "If anyone can help you save your shelter, Shep, it's this guy."

"No doubt about that," Shep said. Then he let out a big sigh. "Well, I gotta load up some more boxes. Nice talking to you, Mr. Bishop."

"Please, call me Richard."

As we watched Shep walk away, my dad turned to me.

"Thinking you can save the shelter is a tiny bit crazy— you know that, right?"

"Yeah," I said sadly.

My dad smiled. "But it's the kind of crazy that makes a parent really proud."

CHAPTER 19

TWO HOURS LATER, when I was done at the shelter, my dad was waiting for me in the parking lot.

"Wanna go get ice cream?"

"Sweet!"

"How was work?"

"Sad."

"I'll bet." After a few seconds, he turned the car radio on. "How about a little music to change the mood?"

A voice came out of the speakers: *This weather report sponsored by the Committee to Reelect Rhonda Murpt.*

And then a different voice:

> *Hi, I'm Rhonda! In my first term as mayor of the great town of Quietville, we've seen many great things happen. Our infrastructure is sound, our businesses are*

thriving, and our community is sleeping
safer and sounder than ever before. But as
great as the last four years have been, the
next four are going to be even better! So I
hope you'll join me on Election Day and
vote!

My dad turned the volume down. "Yeesh, we don't need to be listening to that."

"Election Day?" I asked. "That's not until November."

"In Northport we do it a little differently," my dad explained. "We hold local elections in the spring so they can be their own thing."

"Got it," I said. "What's an infrastructure?"

"Roads, bridges, construction, that kind of stuff."

"Well, she seems like a pretty good mayor, right?"

My dad sighed. "I guess so. But you can't believe everything you hear. Politicians always tell you they're awesome—that's part of their job."

"Oh."

Dad turned the radio to a different station. "Do you want to talk about the shelter thing some more?"

"Not really."

At the ice-cream parlor, I ended up getting mocha chocolate chip.

My dad got sorbet.

FACT: Sorbet is just a fancy word for fake ice cream.

We sat on the bench in front of the store and I ate my cone. It was delicious, but not quite delicious enough to make me forget all the boxes I'd just filled at the shelter.

There are some things even ice cream can't fix.

CHAPTER 20

THE NEXT DAY in math class, all eyes were on Kermit Klondike.

Well, six eyes anyway.

Irwin, Baxter, and I all stared at him as soon as we walked into the classroom. Then, when Ms. Owenby started asking questions about the lesson, we stared some more as Kermit raised his hand. And whenever she called on him, he got every answer right!

Things were getting very suspicious.

Finally, at the end of class, it was time to get our quizzes back. Ms. Owenby made her way through the classroom. "Nice job, Becky," she said to one kid. "Need to pay a little more attention next time, Jason," she said to another. She got to Irwin and didn't need to say anything, because he was amazing at math. She got to me and said, "Good work," before putting down my quiz—seventeen out of twenty. I'll take it! When Ms. Owenby walked over to Baxter's desk, she whispered, "You're always welcome to come in for extra help before the final test, you know that," before putting down his quiz. Baxter didn't even look at it before stuffing it inside his backpack.

Then Ms. Owenby got to Kermit's desk.

"Well," she said with a bright smile. "I'm very impressed, young man. Keep up the good work." She handed Kermit his quiz, and a big grin spread over his face. "YES!" he said loudly. "Perfect score! That's what I'm talkin' about!" Then he high-fived his friend Benjy, who also apparently got a good grade, and the two of them howled like hyenas.

"Easy, you two," Ms. Owenby said. "It's just one quiz. But it's very good work. See what happens when you apply yourself?"

"We sure do," crowed Kermit.

Irwin, Baxter, and I caught each other's eye, and it was clear we were all thinking the same thing.

That clinched it.

After class, we huddled in the hallway, waiting for Daisy. As soon as she joined us, we all started talking to her at once.

"Whoa, whoa!" she said. "One at a time."

"He did it!" Irwin said. "Kermit definitely stole the answer sheet. He knew all the answers in class today and practically danced on the table when he got his quiz back. He's definitely the guy."

"Maybe he's just good at math," Daisy suggested.

We all howled at that one.

"He did badly all year!" Baxter insisted. "Just like me!"

"Well, maybe he decided to buckle down," countered Daisy.

I laughed. "Have you met Kermit?"

"Point taken," Daisy said. "Oh boy. You guys are absolutely, positively, one hundred percent sure?"

"Yup," Irwin said.

"Has to be," Baxter said.

They all turned to me. For some reason I hesitated. "Well, I mean, it's not like we all have actual proof or anything—"

"Oh, come on, Jimmy!" scoffed Irwin. "You're the one who first thought he was the guy! Don't wimp out now! He did it for sure."

Jeez. I *was* right. That sure felt good!

"Let's just go talk to him one more time," Daisy said. "To be sure."

Irwin rolled his eyes but nodded. "Fine."

We walked down the hall, the four of us, and all of a sudden I actually felt kind of cool. We were a gang, we were the CrimeBiters, and we were about to solve a case in front of everybody. We might actually be heroes!

As we rounded a corner, we saw Kermit standing at a water fountain, hanging out with his friend Benjy and another kid, Derek. The three of them were spitting water at each other. Kermit wouldn't get in trouble though, because his father was Mr. Klondike.

When they saw us coming, they straightened up and turned in our direction, with nasty grins on their faces.

"Well, hello, boys and girl," Kermit said. "How can I be of assistance? Did your car need a wash?" Then he splurted some water in Irwin's direction, but luckily it missed.

"That is so gross!" Irwin cried. "I can't wait until you get what you deserve!"

"What are you talking about?" snapped Kermit.

Daisy jumped in before Irwin could say anything else. "Hey, Kermit, I heard you did really well on the math quiz," she said. "That's great."

"Yeah, I did," Kermit said, looking confused. "So what? Since when do you care about my grades?"

"You used to hate math," Baxter said. "Remember? We used to laugh at all the math nerds, for caring about stupid stuff like numbers?"

"Just because I laughed at them doesn't mean I couldn't do it if I tried," Kermit said. "I've always been good at math when I study." Then he slurped some more water and threatened to spit it, and Irwin ducked out of the way. "Ha!" Kermit said, his mouth dribbling nasty little droplets.

"What do you guys want?" asked Benjy. "Like, what are you doing here?"

Some other kids started to gather around. Mara Lloyd, Daisy's chipper friend, was one of the first to arrive. "What's going on, you guys?" she chirped excitedly. "It sounds like you guys are fighting."

"Nothing's going on," grumbled Kermit. "These nimwads are just annoying me, that's all."

Daisy stared at Kermit, as cool as a cucumber. "How are we annoying? We're just congratulating you on your math quiz." She pointed at Baxter, Irwin, and myself. "These guys were really impressed."

"Yeah," I said, "you did better than me."

"Well, whose problem is that?" Kermit sneered. Then he looked at his friends. "Let's go, you guys."

"Not yet," Daisy said. Irwin, Baxter, and I suddenly tensed up. Daisy had always been the bravest one of us all. She was the one who had first confronted Baxter, back when he was a bully just like Kermit. "We just want to know one other thing," Daisy added. "Did you . . . maybe—"

"I'M DONE TALKING TO YOU GUYS!" Kermit yelled, losing his temper. He put his hand in the water fountain and flicked some water in our direction. "SCRAM!"

By now the hallway was pretty clogged with people, and a few teachers had noticed what was going on, since kids were late for their next class. I looked up and saw Ms. Owenby and Mr. Klondike together, walking straight toward us.

Kermit saw them too. "Dad!" he called. "These guys are hassling me! Tell them to leave me alone!"

Mr. Klondike looked shocked, because usually it was the other way around, with Kermit doing the hassling. He stared down at the four of us. "Is this true?" he asked. "Are you children bothering Kermit?"

Irwin looked like he wanted to crawl off the side of the earth. Baxter didn't look quite as terrified as Irwin, but he looked plenty scared. Even Daisy didn't seem able to form any actual words with her actual mouth.

So I decided to step up. I was the founder of the CrimeBiters, after all. It was my duty.

"I'm very sorry to have to report this, sir, but we believe that Kermit was the one who stole the answer sheet."

Everyone in the hallway gasped. Ms. Owenby looked like she swallowed a ghost.

Mr. Klondike's eyes went wide with shock. "Excuse me?"

"It's true," I said, forging ahead. "We wouldn't say anything unless we were totally sure. He was acting really weird when we were talking about it yesterday, and today he got a hundred on his quiz. I feel terrible to have to tell you this, but the evidence is clear."

I noticed Chad Knight shake his head in disappointment. "Tattletale," he murmured, and a bunch of other kids nodded in agreement.

"Hey, we're solving a crime!" Irwin sputtered, finding his voice. But none of the other kids seemed to look at it that way. Even though everyone thought Kermit was scary and obnoxious, they seemed to think that *we* were the bad guys.

FACT: When you're a kid, tattling on someone is pretty much the worst crime there is.

"Chad, you don't understand," I said, but he just shook his head, and I realized that we weren't going to be considered heroes after all.

"Dad!" fumed Kermit. "These guys are lying! You know I would never do that, ever! I'm great at math when I try!"

"I want to believe you, Kermit, I really do." Mr. Klondike looked at his son, and then at Ms. Owenby. "Miriam? Is this possible? Do you think my son could have done this?"

Ms. Owenby had this weird, panicky look on her face, and all of a sudden my forehead started dripping with sweat and I got a sickening feeling in my stomach. Because somehow, I knew what she was going to say before she said it.

"Uh . . . well . . . it turns out the answer sheet wasn't stolen after all," Ms. Owenby said, her voice barely above a whisper. "I—I misplaced it, that's all. It was under some other papers in my office mailbox, where I found it this morning." She looked like she wanted to follow Irwin off the side of the earth, but instead, she somehow managed to look at Mr. Klondike. "In fact, I was just about to tell you, Seymour. I'm so very sorry."

I couldn't even enjoy the fact that Mr. Klondike's first name was Seymour. Instead, I felt the blood drain out of my face, and I'm pretty sure my fellow CrimeBiters felt the same thing.

"HA!" Kermit bellowed in my face. Then he did the same to Irwin, Daisy, and Baxter. "HA! HA! HA!"

"Let's clear the hallway, please," said Mr. Klondike. "Everyone, off to class. Let's go."

Then he turned to the four of us.

"I will need to see all of you in my office after school," he said. "And I will be calling your parents."

He walked off, and Ms. Owenby slinked away, and the rest of the kids scattered, leaving Irwin, Daisy, Baxter, and myself standing there—alone, embarrassed, and ashamed.

A single thought was going through my mind.

I wish it were yesterday.

CHAPTER 21

MR. KLONDIKE'S OFFICE was way too small for four kids and their parents, so we met in the teacher's lounge. There were a bunch of posters of other countries on the wall, almost as if the teachers liked to go in there and close their eyes and imagine they were in India or Kenya, instead of a classroom with a bunch of goody-goody tattletales with overactive imaginations.

My dad was there, and Irwin's mom, and Baxter's mom. Daisy's parents both worked in the city, so she got off parent-free. So lucky.

"Thank you all for coming," Mr. Klondike began. "We spoke on the phone about why you're here, so we don't have to go over all that again. But I thought it was a good idea to discuss with the children how this happened, and why it's so important that it never happen again." His eyes bore in on the four of us. "Would any of you like to begin?"

I was pretty sure he didn't want the honest answer to that question. We shifted uncomfortably in our seats. So did our parents.

"Jimmy, how about you?" Mr. Klondike suggested.

Ugh.

"Er . . . well, it's really bad and wrong to tell on your friends," I said. "Even if they're not technically your friends." *And especially if they're the son of the vice-principal.*

"We're really sorry we did that," Baxter added.

"Totally sorry," Irwin chimed in.

Only Daisy didn't answer.

"Young lady?" Mr. Klondike asked her. "Do you agree with your friends here? Is that why we're all gathered in this room?"

She whispered something so softly that nobody could hear her.

"Could you repeat that?" asked Mr. Klondike.

"I don't think so," she said, slightly louder.

Mr. Klondike nodded. "Correct, Miss Flowers. That is not why we're here. If a student does something wrong or illegal, and you know it beyond a doubt, it *is* in fact your responsibility to alert a teacher or administrator, although I do understand that it may make you unpopular with your peers for a time. But it is the right thing to do."

"Why are we here, then?" Baxter asked.

Mrs. Wonk, who had this look on her face like she had just smelled a dead fish, lifted her head up. "Why don't you answer that, Irwin? Surely you know the answer."

"I do?" Irwin looked around nervously, then cleared his throat. "I guess, maybe, because Kermit is Mr. Klondike's son?"

"NO!" Mr. Klondike said, dropping his pen angrily on the table. "Have we taught you children nothing in this school?"

"I think I know," I said.

All heads turned in my direction.

"It's wrong to accuse somebody of something if you don't know all the facts."

Mr. Klondike took a deep breath and sat down. "Thank you, Mr. Bishop," he said. "You are absolutely correct."

"Good job, son," said my dad, even though he looked incredibly disappointed in me when he said it.

Baxter's mom sat up straighter in her chair. "It's this gang of theirs," she said. "The CrimeBiters."

Mr. Klondike looked puzzled. "I'm sorry, Mrs. Bratford, the what?"

"The CrimeBiters," she repeated.

"That's not fair," said Mrs. Wonk. "The CrimeBiters is a wonderful thing. It's the first time my son has really felt a part of something, and I'm so grateful."

Mrs. Bratford harrumphed. "Yes, well, they practically think they're detectives in the Quietville Police Department, and it's slightly ridiculous, don't you think?"

I didn't blame Mrs. Bratford for not being huge fans of the CrimeBiters, since our first official act of business was to catch her husband stealing my mom's favorite diamond necklace. But still, what she was saying was very upsetting. At least I knew my dad would never agree with her.

"I agree," my dad said.

I stared at him in shock. "What? You do?"

He nodded. "It's great that you have this group of friends," he said. "But as we've discussed before, it can sometimes go too far. You are young children, after all. It's a good idea to remember that every once in a while."

"I agree as well," said Mr. Klondike. "While your aims are noble, it is very important to leave the crime fighting to the police."

"Crime *biting*," Daisy corrected him, very softly.

"That's right," I said. "We named it that because of Abby, my dog. She has helped solve a lot of cases for us."

"I wouldn't go that far," Irwin said.

"I would," I said.

"Here we go again," Baxter said.

"Everyone stop!" Mr. Klondike looked at his watch. "I have a meeting down at the Board of Education, so I'm afraid we must bring this meeting to an end. Thank you all for making the time to come in today." He shook all the parents' hands, then turned to the four of us. We were still sitting in our chairs, waiting for something terrible to happen. Would we be suspended? Have after-school detention for the rest of our lives? Be made to clean the bathrooms for a year?

"You four are free to go," said Mr. Klondike.

We all looked at each other, confused. "We are?" asked Daisy.

"Yes." Mr. Klondike stood directly over us, blocking the light from the fluorescent lamps, almost like a total eclipse of the sun. "I hope you've learned a valuable lesson here today. Good afternoon."

As my dad and I walked to the car, neither of us said a word. Finally, halfway home, he turned to me and asked, "What were you thinking?"

"I was trying to help," I said.

"It is important to do the right thing," he said. "But it is more important to do the correct thing."

I stared out the window. "I'm really sorry, Dad."

He sighed. "It's okay, as long as you've learned something. You don't need to be a hero all the time. I know you're trying to be like that guy in *STOP! POLICE!*, or that vampire in those books you love, but you're forgetting one important thing."

I looked at him. "What's that?"

My dad sighed. "They're not real."

CHAPTER 22

DINNER THAT NIGHT was not fun.

The not-fun part began as soon we sat down, when my mom said, "Your father and I have been talking."

FACT: Whenever your mom starts with "Your father and I have been talking," you can be pretty sure that the rest of the conversation is not going to be good.

"Uh-oh," said Misty, who was staring at her phone.

"No devices at dinner," my dad told her.

"But—" Misty began. Then she looked up, saw the expressions on my parents' faces, and quickly put her phone away.

My mom continued. "I heard about what happened at school today, and obviously I'm very disappointed. There are few things more serious than accusing somebody of doing something that they didn't do."

"I know that," I mumbled.

"Do you?" My mom put her fork down, which was a sign that she really meant business. "I feel like you're more concerned with proving to everybody what a brilliant detective you are. Well, I have news for you, Jimmy. You're eleven years old. Most detectives are quite a bit older than you."

"Like by thirty years," Misty said, as if I didn't get the point.

"Jimmy," said my dad. "We know how much the CrimeBiters means to you. We really do. But we need to put the brakes on this whole thing for a little while."

I wasn't quite sure what I was hearing. "What?" I said. "Are you serious? You want me to stop hanging out with my best friends?"

"Of course not," my mom said. "We think it's great that you have such close friends. But this idea you have, that the club's main objective is solving crimes—that's what we're concerned about. Why can't you just be a normal group of friends, who do normal, group-of-friends things?"

"Are you serious?" I asked desperately. "You want me to be normal? You're the ones who are always telling me to be my own person, to stand out, to not feel like I have to be like everyone else!"

"Standing out is great," my dad said. "Standing out for the wrong reasons is not."

"FORGET YOU GUYS!" I lurched out of my chair. "Come on, Abby. Let's go for a walk."

"Sit down, please," said my mom, but I pretended not to hear. Abby followed me as we went outside. I put her leash on and we walked for twenty minutes until I found myself in front of the Boathouse. I stood there and stared at the place where the gang was formed, and where we had our meetings. It used to be the best thing ever. How did it all go so wrong?

I bent down and petted Abby. "I'm sorry, girl." She licked my hand.

Then I realized it was going to be dark soon, so I took a deep breath.

"Let's go home," I told Abby.

We ran all the way.

PART THREE

THE ULTIMATE TEST

CHAPTER 23

"WHAT DO YOU guys want to do?"

I was at Baxter's house after school, watching Baxter do yet another math problem. Irwin was sitting next to him, drumming his fingers on the table, waiting for him to finish. Daisy was reading a book and kicking her legs into the back of my chair, trying to annoy me. It was working.

"What do you guys want to do?" I repeated, since no one answered me the first time.

Daisy looked at me. "What do you mean? We're helping Baxter."

"I'm really starting to get the hang of it," Baxter said.

Irwin rolled his eyes. "Do you think maybe you could get the hang of it any faster?"

"I meant after," I said. "We're going to be done tutoring Baxter soon, and we need something to do before dinner."

I didn't have to say it, because it was obvious: ever since the whole Kermit Klondike disaster, we were all a little nervous about doing any CrimeBiters stuff.

I looked down at Abby, who was lying at my feet. Even *she* looked bored. I almost wished Daisy had brought Purrkins, because at least it would have provided a little excitement. But it turns out cats never really leave the house they live in. Isn't that crazy?

FACT: I would not want to be a cat.

"Don't you have your volunteer thing at the shelter?" Irwin asked. "It's Thursday, don't you usually go there on Thursdays?"

I shook my head sadly. "Not anymore, now that Shep has to close the shelter."

"Ugh," Daisy said sadly. "That stinks."

"You're telling me." I got up and stretched my legs, just to have something to do. Abby got up and stretched her legs too. We looked at each other like, *Now what?*

And then, from one second to the next, I had an answer to that question.

"Maybe you guys can help me save it."

Baxter looked up from his scribbling. "Help you save what?"

"The shelter." I started walking around his kitchen as I got more excited by the idea. "When I told my dad that I wanted to help Shep keep the shelter, he looked at me like I was crazy. But there has to be a way, right?"

Daisy got up and started pacing with me. "And technically, it wouldn't be a CrimeBiters activity, because we wouldn't be solving a crime, right? We would be helping a person with their business."

Irwin looked skeptical, as usual. "Hold on a second. Didn't you say that Shep sold the shelter?"

I nodded. "Something like that. It was Shep's business but he didn't own the building. The guy who does is selling it to some other people who are turning it into a shopping center."

"Well, then," Daisy said, "the first thing we have to do is figure out who bought it, and talk them out of it."

I shook my head. "I asked Shep about that. Apparently it's some investment company that wants to stay private."

"Of course they do, but we can figure it out anyway!" Daisy said excitedly.

"Really?" I asked, feeling a slight flurry of hope.

Irwin snorted out a laugh. "You want to stop some zillionaires from buying a building? Good luck with that."

"Irwin!" I said, sharply enough to get everyone's attention. "Why do you have to be so negative all the time? All you ever say is why we can't do something! Why can't you be positive for once?"

"Okay, fine," Irwin snapped back. "I'm positive you can't do anything to help Shep. He doesn't even own the building, for crying out loud!"

"I think Irwin might be right," Daisy said. "And your dad and Shep and everyone else too. A deal's a deal, and there's no real way to stop it."

"UGH!" I flopped back down onto one of Baxter's chairs and stared at the wall. There was a picture of Baxter's parents, which was always weird to look at, since his dad was Barnaby Bratford, famous Quietville jewelry thief. He was in jail somewhere. We didn't talk about it with Baxter very much, but we knew he went to go see his dad every other weekend.

Which gave me an idea.

"Hey, Baxter," I said. "When are you going to visit your dad next?"

Baxter blinked. "Um . . . this Sunday. Why?"

"Can I come?"

They all looked at me like I was crazy.

"Um, I'll have to ask my mom, but I guess so," Baxter said. "But, uh . . . why would you want to?"

I hesitated before answering. "Because if anyone knows the best way to take something from someone else," I said, "it's probably him."

WHEN I'D TOLD my parents I wanted to go visit Mr. Bratford, they didn't say anything for a full two minutes. Finally, my dad looked at my mom, who nodded.

And then she said, "Okay."

So on Sunday, I found myself heading to the state prison.

At the beginning of the drive there—it was pretty far, almost two hours—Baxter's mom asked me a question: "Are you sure about this?" When I said yes, she just nodded and turned on the radio.

Mrs. Cragg was with us too. She was Mr. Bratford's sister, and the minute I told her my plan, she said she wanted to come. I didn't try to stop her. I was kind of glad, to tell you the truth.

I guess I fell asleep in the car, because as soon as we pulled up to the giant gate in front, I woke up and saw Mrs. Bratford looking straight at me.

"Just about time to go inside," she said.

Now, you probably could have guessed this already, but I've never been to a prison before. I've seen a lot of them on TV, but this one was a lot different. For one thing, it was huge. For another, there was no way you could tell it was a prison from the outside. It looked more like a really ugly hotel.

But the main thing was, it was really quiet. No shouting or rattling of bars or anything like that. It almost felt like a library, but the people weren't there because they liked reading. They were there because they liked breaking the law.

When we arrived, we were led into a room that looked kind of like a cafeteria, except there was no food. Just a bunch of tables, and benches, and a few guards standing around, keeping an eye on things. We sat down at one of the tables and waited. And waited, and waited, and waited some more.

"It's always like this," Baxter explained. "We have to get here at an exact time but then we wait for a while before Dad comes."

I wasn't sure I'd ever heard him call his dad "Dad" before.

Finally, after about twenty more minutes, the door opened and Barnaby Bratford came in. He looked completely different than the last time I'd seen him, when he was lying with a broken back on the Boathouse floor. For one thing, he now had a black-haired wig to cover up his bald head. For another, he'd shaved his beard.

But the most amazing difference was, he looked small. And lost.

Believe it or not, I actually felt a little sorry for him.

He stuck out his hand, and I shook it.

We all stood there in silence for a minute, until Mrs. Cragg said, "Barnaby, I'm sure you remember Jimmy. He's a terrific young man, and he wanted to come up here and see you."

"So it's true," he said. "You really did want to visit me. I'm very surprised. But also grateful."

I wasn't sure what to say to that, so I didn't say anything.

"It gives me a chance to apologize to you in person," continued Mr. Bratford. "I was on a wrong path there for a while. A terribly wrong path. But I've found my way back to the right one."

"It's true," Baxter said softly. "My dad is a different person now."

"That's great, sir," I said.

"How is your dog?" Mr. Bratford asked.

"Very good, sir," I answered.

He laughed, a little sadly. "Young man, please don't call me sir. I certainly haven't done anything to earn that." He hugged Baxter for a quick second, then looked back at me. "I'm so happy that you've become friends with my son. I've heard all about your adventures together."

"We're called the CrimeBiters," Baxter said.

"Well, I can certainly see where that name comes from." Mr. Bratford tried to smile, but I saw him wince, which reminded me that the last time I saw him, he had just crashed through a hole in the roof and fallen twenty feet.

"Are you all right, Mr. Bratford? I mean, is your back better?"

He nodded slowly. "Well, to be perfectly honest with you, Jimmy, it still causes me a bit of pain every now and again. But I accept it. It reminds me of where I came from, who I was, and who I never want to be again."

I nodded, and he nodded, and it seemed like that was all there was to say on that subject.

Mrs. Cragg cleared her throat. "Jimmy has something he'd like to ask you, Barnaby," she said. "Go ahead, Jimmy."

"Well, sir—I mean, Mr. Bratford—this might sound really strange, but I'd like your advice."

"That does sound strange," Mr. Bratford agreed, and everyone laughed awkwardly.

"The thing is, my friend runs an animal shelter downtown," I said. "He is being kicked out because the guy who owns the building sold it to some people who are turning it into a shopping center. I was wondering if you had any advice on how to stop that from happening."

"Why would you think I could help?" Mr. Bratford asked.

I took a deep breath. "Well, because I know you used to own a business and you might know—uh—how to, you know—how the system works?"

Mr. Bratford's eyes crinkled up, and he actually laughed, for the first time. "Well, now, hold on. Are you saying you want to know if there's a way that you can maybe bend the rules a little bit?"

"Oh gosh, no!" I said quickly. "But . . . is there a way to prevent something like this from happening?"

"Well, the old me might have suggested one thing," Mr. Bratford said, still smiling a bit. "But the new me suggests something else entirely. You need to go talk to the only people who are even more sneaky than crooks."

We all leaned forward in our chairs.

"Who's that?" Baxter asked.

"The politicians," said Barnaby Bratford.

CHAPTER 25

WHICH IS HOW Baxter and I ended up in Mayor Rhonda Murpt's office the very next day.

It was an impressive office, by the way. Mayor Murpt was the mayor of a pretty small town, but she had a big, beautiful office, with wood paneling on the walls, a huge couch with flower-patterned pillows all over it, and a desk the size of a car. It didn't feel very office-y. It kind of looked like the home study of a super rich, super important person.

"Whoa," said Baxter. "This place is sweet."

Earlier that afternoon I'd called and found out that the mayor had public office hours every afternoon from four to five, so I made an appointment for 4:15. Then I called Baxter to meet me downtown. I told Mrs. Cragg I was going to the skate park, because I was pretty sure she wouldn't be thrilled with the idea of my taking Abby to the mayor's office.

"The skate park?" Mrs. Cragg had said. "But you don't skate."

"I'm thinking of learning."

"Hmmm," she'd said, like she wasn't quite sure whether or not to believe me, but she still let me go.

On our way to see the mayor, Baxter asked if we should invite Daisy and Irwin, but I shook my head. "Irwin will laugh and say it's a terrible idea, as usual. And Daisy was pretty convinced we were wasting our time, remember?" I had a brief moment of doubt, but I wished it away. "Let's just see what happens, and we can fill them in later."

FACT: It's decisions like this that usually come back to haunt you.

When we got to city hall, the first person we saw was a security guard who was chomping on a cheeseburger. He took one look at Abby and said, "No dogs."

Little did he know, I'd done my homework. "Isn't this a public building?" I asked. "Aren't you public servants? And aren't we the public?"

The guard was a little too shocked by my confidence to say anything.

"That's what I thought," I added. "There is no law that says a member of the public can't bring his pet to this building. So please, let us pass."

In the lobby, we saw people with cameras, hanging around like they were waiting for something to happen. One woman saw Abby and raised her eyebrows, but the rest of them just looked at us and yawned. I guess we weren't all that interesting.

Meanwhile, the guard decided we'd interrupted his cheeseburger long enough. "Just don't let that dog make a mess," he said with his mouth full, as we waited for the elevator.

"Oh, she would never do that," I said, just as Abby sniffed a man's leg suspiciously. "Stop that!" I whispered loudly. She stopped. Phew.

When we got upstairs, a well-dressed woman met us at the elevator. "You're here to see Mayor Murpt?"

"We are," I said. "We have an appointment."

TIP: Never show up at the mayor's office unannounced.

The woman looked us up and down, especially Abby. "Wait here, please."

Abby examined the lady's foot and then let out a little sound, halfway between a yip and a growl. "We must vet our appointments more thoroughly," the woman mumbled to herself as she walked away.

"Vet?" asked Baxter.

"Short for veterinarian," I said. (Which was totally incorrect. I found out later it means "examine carefully.")

We sat down and waited. I glanced up at the walls, which were covered with pictures of a woman who must have been Mayor Murpt, posing with semi-famous local people, like the high school girl who won the state championship in the mile run, and the guy who broke the world record for pogo stick jumping.

Finally, we heard a loud, extra chipper voice. "It's not every day I get a visit from two schoolchildren. And their little dog too! How wonderful!"

We all looked up and saw a very small, very thin woman in a yellow dress walking toward us. Two inches behind her was a guy in a suit, who looked barely older than Misty's boyfriend, staring at his cell phone.

"I'm Rhonda Murpt," she said, holding out both her hands. "It's so good to see you here today." She gestured at the guy behind her, who nodded at us. "And this is my chief of staff, Eric Miranda. He keeps the trains running on time."

"What trains?" I asked.

She laughed. "So adorable! My youngest constituents are my most valuable, for it is you kids that will keep our democracy thriving for generations to come. And who's this?" she asked, looking down.

"Her name's Abby," I said.

"Well, hello, little Abby," said the mayor, and she bent down to scratch Abby's back. Abby doesn't love getting her back scratched though, so she let out a little growl.

"Oh gosh," said Mayor Murpt. "I didn't hurt her, did I?"

"Of course not," I said. Then to Abby I hissed, "Be nice."

"Come in, come in!" the mayor chirped, and we all followed her into the office. She pointed at the big flowery couch. "Please sit! Can I get you children anything to drink? Some juice?"

PROFILE

Name: Rhonda Murpt

Age: Not sure, but I'm pret[ty]
sure her hair was dyed

Occupation: Mayor

Interests: Running the tow[n]
getting re-elected so she c[an]
keep running the town

PROFILE

Name: Eric Miranda

Age: Way too young to act like
such a big shot

Occupation: Mayor's assistant

Interests: Helping the mayor
look mayoral

I said no, but Baxter asked for apple juice. As soon as it came, I was mad that I hadn't asked for juice too.

Mayor Murpt's phone rang. She glanced at it, decided to ignore it, and looked up at us with a bright smile. "So, do you mind if I ask where your parents are?"

Baxter and I looked at each other, neither of us sure what to say. Finally Baxter said, "We wanted it to be a surprise," which seemed like a good answer, even though I wasn't quite sure what the *it* would turn out to be.

"I see." Mayor Murpt put on her best business face, even though I could tell she was wondering what the heck she was doing sitting there with two children. "And how can I help you kids?"

"Well," I said, "we wanted to know if you could help us. The shelter where I volunteer and where I adopted Abby is going to close in a few weeks because the person who owns it sold it to some other people who want to tear down the building and turn it into a big shopping center."

Mayor Murpt's smile faded for a second, but she recovered quickly. "Whoa there, slow down just a minute," she said. "A shelter? An animal shelter?"

"Yes, ma'am," I said. "Northport Animal Rescue Foundation. Most people call it Northport ARF. It's run by a man named Shep Lansing."

"And they also have training for pets," Baxter added. "Abby trained there. She used to eat all of Jimmy's mom's shoes, but now she's a lot better."

"Can you help us?" I asked the mayor. "Can you stop the sale of the shelter? Someone told us that the town can step in if it's for the public good."

"Well, now, that's a very interesting question," said Mayor Murpt. "Of course, a government is able and, in fact, required to protect the rights of its citizens. But it cannot overstep its bounds and impinge on the rights of its citizens either. That would not be in the best interests of our democracy."

"Impinge?" Baxter asked.

"Interfere with," Eric Miranda clarified.

"Correct," said the mayor. "I am happy to look into this situation, but I'm not sure there's anything I can do." She snuck a quick look at her watch. "Well, thank you so much for stopping by. You really are terrific kids. The future of our city and our nation is in good hands!"

She got to her feet, and Mr. Miranda leaped up to stand behind her.

"So you really can't do anything to help?" I asked. "You're just going to let all those poor cats and dogs and bunnies get thrown out into the street?"

"As I said, it's a private matter," the mayor said, already looking at her phone. "The government cannot step in. I do wish I had better news."

I felt deflated. "Come on, Baxter," I said. "Let's go tell Shep."

I bent down and woke Abby up from her nap. She stretched, yawned, and then for some reason let out a real growl. I even saw some fang.

I hadn't seen her fangs in three weeks. I'd almost forgotten how big they were.

"Abby!" I said. "Stop that!"

The mayor laughed. "Oh, it's okay," she said. "She's probably just smelling my dog."

As we headed for the door, I heard Mr. Miranda say, "Madame Mayor, do you mind if I talk to you for a minute?" Then he looked at us and said, "Hold up just a minute, guys."

As they talked quietly in a corner, Abby kept staring

at them. She was making a very soft sound, and it wasn't the friendly type.

I tugged on her leash. "Stop embarrassing me in front of the mayor."

I was getting more and more nervous that something bad was going to happen, but two seconds later the mayor walked over to us with a big smile on her face.

"Eric thinks it would be a nice idea to get a few pictures, which we can put on our website and release to the press," Mayor Murpt said. "I agree, it would set a terrific example for other youngsters, seeing us together—we can show them that it's never too early to care about your community."

Baxter and I looked at each other. "A picture?" I asked. "With us?"

"That's right," Eric Miranda said. "We'll tweet it out to all her followers. Now, if you two wouldn't mind, I'd like you to stand over here."

Mr. Miranda spoke quietly into his phone. Two seconds later, the door opened, and all the people we'd seen at the front door of the building rushed in, with cameras and laptops and notebooks. The next thing I knew, we were all gathered by the big wooden desk, right next to two giant American flags on two poles, posing for pictures.

"Why don't you pick Abby up?" Mr. Miranda suggested. "Might make for a better optic."

"Okay," I said, even though I had no idea what *optic* meant. Abby wasn't exactly thrilled about getting scooped up, but she didn't fight me either.

FLASH! FLASH! FLASH! Baxter and I were excited to pose for the various cameras, already planning what we'd say to all the jealous kids back at school. But then I got a pit in my stomach as I suddenly realized that Daisy and Irwin would be two of those kids.

"Ah yes, ladies and gentlemen of the press," said Mayor Murpt. "So glad to have you here with us. I'm very happy to welcome these youngsters here today to learn about government."

"What were the kids doing here?" shouted out one guy with a camera.

"New campaign managers?" another yelled, and everyone laughed.

"Just two curious kids wanting to learn," Eric Miranda

interrupted. "And please, no policy questions. Just pictures."

The camera people took their pictures, but most of them looked pretty bored.

"Typical photo op," one mumbled.

"Photo op?" Baxter asked.

The mayor chuckled. "Photo opportunity," she said. "Which is one of the most important duties of any politician."

The cameras snapped away. My mouth was getting tired from smiling.

"How many more pictures?" I asked, to no one in particular.

A woman with red hair and a notebook laughed. "Not too many," she said. "Pretty cool being in the mayor's office though, isn't it?"

"Totally cool," I said. "The mayor is so nice. Even though she couldn't really help us."

"Help you with what?" she asked.

"We were trying to save the shelter downtown, but I guess there's nothing we can do."

A guy with a camera glanced over in my direction.

"The animal shelter?" asked another guy. "With all the cats and dogs? What's happening to it?"

"Thanks, everyone!" said Eric Miranda. "I think we have everything we need."

But the press people had woken up.

They started asking questions, even though Mr. Miranda kept repeating, "No questions, please," and, "This is not a news conference."

Finally, Mayor Murpt held up her hand. "It's true. These young children have asked if there's any way to block the sale of a building downtown, and we've explained how in a democratic society, government is not allowed to prevent a private business transaction."

"How about a petition?" said the red-haired woman with the notebook.

All heads turned toward her. "A petition?" I asked.

"Yup," she said. "Isn't that something they can try, Mayor Murpt?"

The mayor froze for a second, then smiled brightly. "Well, technically it is true that you could bring a petition to the next Zoning Board meeting and the committee will discuss it. But they very rarely overturn this kind of thing."

I yanked Abby's leash tight so she wouldn't try any funny business. "But it's something we can try? I mean, it's worth a shot, right?"

The mayor looked at the lady with red hair, then down at me. "Yes, of course."

Mr. Miranda nodded. "I'm sure the public would be very impressed with such civic-minded youngsters, taking action after getting valuable advice from the mayor."

As the cameras kept clicking away, Baxter elbowed

me in the ribs. "This is so cool," he said. "We're gonna be famous!"

I looked at the mayor. "Thanks," I said. "For changing your mind about helping us."

"She's a politician," said the red-haired lady. "They change their minds all the time."

CHAPTER 26

AS SOON AS I got home, my mom announced that we were going to the farmer's market. "They're just starting summer Mondays!" she said happily.

"But I have a lot of other stuff I have to do," I complained, thinking about the petition for Shep's shelter that I wanted to start.

My mom frowned. "This is one of the things we always do together," she said, and I immediately felt bad. She works really hard, and I know it makes her sad sometimes that she doesn't get to spend more time with me.

"Okay, Mom," I said.

"Plus, you can visit Isaac," she said, knowing that would perk me up. Isaac's chocolate chip cookies were the best I'd ever tasted.

As we pulled out of the driveway, I saw Abby glaring

across the street, toward Daisy's house. Purrkins was at the window, glaring back. The tension was so thick, you could cut it with a knife.

"Seriously, you two?" I said. "Are you guys ever going to get over it?" Abby glanced over at me, then went back to her staring contest. She kept at it until we were at least three streets away.

On the way to the market, I told my mom about going to the mayor's office and how I was going to start a petition to try and stop the sale of the shelter. She looked a little shocked.

"You actually went down to the mayor's office? By yourself?"

"Well, with Baxter, my fellow CrimeBiter," I said, hoping to get a few extra brownie points for the gang, which might come in handy later.

"Wow. That's impressive. But I kind of wish you'd told me and your dad beforehand."

"Why?"

She glanced over at me from behind the wheel. "Because."

"*Because* is not a complete sentence."

"Watch it, wise guy."

I glanced in the rearview mirror and saw Abby's snout getting smacked around by the wind.

FACT: There are very few things dogs like more than sticking their head out the window of a moving car.

When we turned into the market, Abby knew exactly where we were and proceeded to yowl with excitement.

FACT: I'm not sure *yowl* is a word, but if it isn't, it should be.

As soon as we piled out of the car, my mom went one way and Abby and I went another—straight toward Isaac's cookie stand.

"My friends!" he cried, standing there surrounded by delicious-looking baked goods of all shapes and sizes—cookies, cakes, muffins, and some other weird half-cookie-half-muffin things called scones. The smell was overpoweringly perfect.

"Hey, Isaac," I said, but he wasn't paying attention to me. He was down on one knee, scratching Abby's right ear. Abby was making a happy noise. I think Isaac was too.

PROFILE

Name: Isaac Baker (okay, fine, I made the last name up)

Age: Old enough to know how to create the perfect cookie

Occupation: Cookie maker

Interests: Combining chocolate, butter, sugar, and flour into bite-size pieces of heaven

"My mom said I could get a dozen cookies," I told Isaac, and he stretched himself back up to his very large height and pulled a paper bag from beneath his table.

"All chocolate chip?"

"All chocolate chip."

As I waited, another shopper wandered over to Isaac's cookie stand. After a minute though, it felt like she was inspecting me just as much as the yummy treats. Abby noticed her staring at me too, and gave out a tiny little growl.

Finally, the woman stepped forward and said, "Do I know you?"

I shook my head. "I don't think so."

But she kept staring. Then she slapped her hand on her forehead and said, "Of course! You're one of the kids from the picture."

By now Isaac was listening too. "What picture?" he said.

The woman took out her phone and punched a few buttons. "Here, look," she said, handing me the phone. On the homepage of a website called QuietvilleToday.com there was a picture of me, Abby, and Baxter with Mayor Murpt.

The caption said: *COMMUNITY KIDS TAKE ACTION!* Then underneath it said: *Two young Quietville students visit Mayor Murpt, asking for advice on civic affairs. "It's so gratifying to see these youngsters participating in local government," said the mayor. "We can all learn from their sense of responsibility, no matter how old we are!"*

"You're famous!" said the lady. "And good for you, young man. Your parents must be very proud."

"Thanks, I hope so," I said, handing the phone back to her. "I was there trying to save the animal shelter. I wonder why the mayor left that part out."

"Wow," said Isaac. "Very cool, Jimmy."

"We're going to start a petition," I told him. "If we get enough names, we can take it to the Zoning Board and see if they'll stop the sale."

Isaac grinned. "Well, you know the best way to get someone to sign a petition, right?" He picked up a box of his cookies. "Baked goods, my friend. Baked goods."

Abby started barking in agreement—or maybe because she just wanted a cookie.

"You mean, give people a free cookie?" I asked.

"Let's not get crazy," Isaac said. "Almost free. Have a bake sale with nice, low prices, then while they're shopping, hit them with the petition." He grinned. "People will sign anything after a good cookie."

"What are you two talking about?" said my mom, who had just walked up with two bags full of vegetables. (So, so wrong.)

"I'm teaching your son to embrace his inner activist," Isaac said. "Step one: how to get what you want."

"Oh boy," my mom said, rolling her eyes. "Please don't give him any crazy ideas."

"It's all good!" Isaac picked up a cookie from the table. "Here, Sarah, try one of today's specials: a coconut chocolate chip peanut butter muffin top."

As soon as Mom bit into the treat, all was forgiven.

THE NEXT DAY was one of the last tutoring sessions for Baxter before our math final, and we were all supposed to meet at Daisy's house. The first thing I saw when I walked across the street was Purrkins snoozing by the front door. I bent down and scratched her belly.

"Hey, Purrky," I said. "That's going to be my nickname for you, okay? Purrky."

Purrkins purred happily.

"So, are you and Abby ever going to become friends?" I asked her.

I scratched her for a few more seconds, then went into the house, where Baxter was sitting at the kitchen table being drilled by Irwin.

"How many degrees in a right angle?"

"Ninety."

"How many sides to an octagon?"

"Eight."

"What's your favorite flavor ice cream?"

"Not funny, Irwin."

Irwin threw up his hands. "I can't think of any more questions!" he said. "I think you're ready! You got this!"

Baxter looked shocked. "You really think so?"

"Yup." Irwin noticed me, which gave him the opening he needed. "You're going to get a better grade on this test than Jimmy, that's for sure."

Before I had a chance to insult him back, Daisy came into the room. She had a laptop computer in her hand, and she didn't look happy.

"Look what my mom showed me when I got home from school today," she said, getting right to the point. "You and Baxter went to talk to the mayor? Without us?"

Uh-oh.

Irwin looked confused. "Huh?"

Daisy took the computer over to Irwin and showed him the picture, and his eyes went wide. He got up and started pacing around the kitchen. "Are you kidding me? Is this about trying to save the shelter? What happened to the four of us doing things together?"

"I asked Baxter, and he said he asked you about inviting us," Daisy said, "but you said no."

I glared at Baxter. He looked at me like, *What could I do? She's a girl.*

"Irwin, you always hate all my ideas!" I said. "And Daisy, you agreed with him, and said there wasn't anything anyone could do! So I just figured, what the heck."

She rolled her eyes at me. "You didn't even tell us about this at school today. Chicken."

I had no response to that, because she was absolutely right.

Irwin sat down in a huff. "So, now you guys get to be the famous heroes, and get your picture taken with the mayor, and we're supposed to, what, just be your background singers?"

"Background singers?" Baxter mumbled to himself, thoroughly confused.

"I said I'm sorry," I said. "But can we not argue about this now? We're having a bake sale, so we can gather enough signatures on a petition to ask the town to save the shelter. I would really love it if we could all do it together."

Irwin shook his head. "I doubt it. I have to study." That was ridiculous; ever since I'd known him, he'd been a straight-A student without even trying.

"Believe it or not, Jimmy, I do want to help," Daisy said. "Because I adopted a pet from Shep, just like you." My heart soared, but she sent it crashing back down to earth with her next sentence. "So I would consider participating in the bake sale, but only if I get to bring Purrkins."

I threw my hands up. "I thought you said she never leaves the house!"

"We would make an exception for this," Daisy said.

Here we go again.

I started playing with the laces on my sneakers, in order to avoid looking at her. "Are you serious? You know that Purrkins and Abby don't really like each other, right? No one will stop and talk to us—no matter how good the cookies are—if we have two animals snarling at each other the whole time."

"Well, it's up to you," she said. "If you want my help, we're going to have to figure this thing out."

"I agree with Daisy," Irwin said, completely unsurprisingly.

FACT: The last time Irwin took my side in an argument with Daisy was . . . wait, let me think . . . NEVER.

"Whatever," I said. "Then I'll do it without you guys."

"You can invite your new best friend, the mayor," Irwin said. "And let us know how it all works out."

"When you go to college," I asked Irwin, "are you going to major in being annoying?"

"Can you guys knock it off?" Baxter said, finally. "The test is coming up and the last thing I need is to listen to everyone fighting all the time."

"You're totally right, Baxter," I said. "Which is why I'm leaving."

"Fine," Irwin said. "But don't come running to us when you don't get enough signatures on your stupid petition!"

I started to leave, then turned back.

"Good luck on the test, Baxter."

I think he said "Thanks," but I couldn't be sure, because I was already in the front yard, heading home.

CHAPTER 28

GUESS WHAT?

It turns out Mr. Klondike is a dog lover.

I found that out in school the next day, when he came up to me at lunch and said, "I was very pleased to see the picture of you and Baxter with the mayor."

I put my sandwich down and stared up at him. "You were?"

"I was. I wish more of our students would follow your example and become involved with local government."

I looked across the cafeteria, where Daisy and Irwin were sitting with Daisy's friend Mara. I wasn't sure where Baxter was.

Mr. Klondike sat down next to me, which I think might have been the first time he ever sat with any student in the cafeteria. Other kids pretended not to stare, but that just made it more obvious that they were. "May I ask what it was you were discussing with the mayor?"

I felt like I was under a microscope. I was still getting over the fact that the other kids thought I was a tattle-tale; I didn't really need them thinking I was a teacher's pet too. Or even worse, a vice-principal's pet.

"I want to try and save the animal shelter downtown," I told Mr. Klondike. "I was asking if she could help."

He smiled, which didn't happen very often. "Well, that's terrific." Then he took out his phone. "I want to show you something," he said, scrolling through his pictures until he found what he was looking for. "Ah, here we go," he said, handing the phone to me. I looked—there was a picture of a dog with only three legs. "This is Alvin. I got him at the shelter near where I used to teach. They told me he'd been found in a dumpster, looking for scraps. His leg had been mangled in some kind of accident, so we had to have it amputated. But we've had Alvin for almost nine years now, and he's a great dog. Kermit loves him to death, don't you, son?"

I looked up and saw Kermit standing over us. I hadn't even noticed him walk up. "Yup," Kermit said, looking at the floor.

"Hey, Kermit," I said. "I'm having a bake sale on Saturday, where I'm going to start a petition to save the animal shelter downtown. Do you want to come?"

Kermit blinked in surprise. "You want my help?"

"Yeah, that'd be awesome."

"Um, okay, maybe," Kermit said, shuffling his feet. "What do I have to do?"

"Get signatures, and sell cookies." I grinned. "Maybe eat a few too."

"I can probably do that."

Mr. Klondike got up. "Well, I'll leave you two to it," he said. "I will make an announcement about your bake sale tomorrow, and if you make flyers, the school can pass them out for the students to take home. I think we can help you get a good turnout."

He started to walk away, but I tapped him on the arm, and he turned back. "Yes, Mr. Bishop?"

"I—I just wanted to say again to you and Kermit that I'm really sorry about what happened last week. I made a bad mistake."

"I understand," Mr. Klondike said.

But I wasn't finished. "Not just about Kermit though." I hesitated. "About you too."

He frowned. "How so?"

"I was always scared of you," I told him. "But now—I think I'm not scared anymore."

Mr. Klondike smiled. "People can surprise you some-times. You just have to give them a chance. Isn't that right, Kermit?"

Kermit nodded but didn't say anything.

"I can't wait to meet Alvin," I said to Kermit. "Can you bring him to the bake sale?"

"I guess," he said. "He loves cookies."

"So does Abby," I told him.

Kermit smiled a little.

And just like that, things felt different.

It's not like we were suddenly best friends or anything.

But it was a start.

CHAPTER 29

YOU KNOW WHAT the good thing about a bake sale is? It makes everything smell like cookies.

"Isaac, you've outdone yourself," said my dad, as we all stood in front of the Quietville town green. "These cookies are magnificent."

"Thanks, chief," Isaac said. He called most adult males "chief."

I looked around at all the people who came to help: Baxter, my parents, my sister, Chad Knight, a few of the guys from the lacrosse team. Shep had brought Kelsey, who was also busy sampling Isaac's treats.

"Your mum is right," she said. "These are gorgeous."

"Who calls food gorgeous?" I asked.

Kelsey licked her fingers. "Civilized people, that's who."

Shep came over, popped a cookie in his mouth, then gave me a big hug. "Jimmy, this is radical!"

"It's what?"

"Radical!" He waved his arms in a big circle. "You're, like, an inspiration, dude. You're taking on big business, fighting back through peaceful protest. It didn't even occur to me to do this, but you . . ." His face got very serious all of a sudden. "You're taking on the MAN. And you're a KID." He almost looked like he was going to cry for a second. "I'm sorry, but that's intense, dude."

"Thanks," I said, not really knowing what he was talking about. "I just want to help the animals."

"Radical," Shep repeated. Then he walked away, smiling and shaking his head.

I turned and was semishocked to see Kermit Klondike walking up, just like he said he would, carrying a big Tupperware container in one hand and Alvin's leash in the other.

"Wow, you really came." I looked down at Alvin, who was pretty tiny. "Hey there, little guy. Boy, are you cute!"

"Did you bring Abby?" Kermit asked.

I shook my head. "Nah, not today. Too much to do, and she can be pretty, uh, distracting sometimes."

He held out the container. "Applesauce muffins. My dad made them."

Whoa. It was hard enough getting used to the fact that Mr. Klondike was actually a nice person who loved dogs. But a *baker* of *muffins*? That was almost too much to handle.

"Great!" I said. "It would be awesome if you could just put them over there next to Isaac's brownie marshmallow surprise."

Mayor Murpt surprised us by coming down to the bake sale, and she brought Eric Miranda with her (I think she brought him everywhere). She also brought a camera crew and a big sign that said RE-ELECT RHONDA!

"When I met young Jimmy Bishop in my office, I immediately recognized that this was a young man who cared," the mayor told people who were hanging out on the green. "A young man who wanted to make a difference in our lives, and our precious animals' lives. So I urge you to stop by his booth, sign his petition, and have a cookie while you're at it!"

"Isn't she gonna say my name?" muttered Isaac. "I could use the plug."

"Have a wonderful day!" declared Mayor Murpt, and she walked off to extremely scattered applause. Then she got into a really sweet, powder-blue BMW, which made me wonder for a second how much mayors of small towns were paid.

"That was really nice of her," I said. "Why didn't people clap louder?"

"Because she's a politician," Shep said, as if that explained everything.

Baxter, Chad, and Kermit were in charge of handing out the flyers, and they were doing a solid job. "Best cookies ever, fifty cents for three!" they crowed. "You know you want 'em!" Whenever someone walked up to our table, Isaac handled the sale, and either Shep or I would hit them up with the petition. "Help save the shelter!" we'd say. "The animals need your help! Please protect the puppies and kittens!"

Who could turn that down?

Sure enough, people started to wander over, just a few at first, then a steady trickle, and after about half an hour, it was a nonstop flow. According to my mom, we needed four hundred signatures to be able to take the petition to the Zoning Board meeting—which seemed like a ton. But it soon became clear that we'd reach that number in no time.

"Wow!" I said to Isaac. "We're gonna sell out!"

"Those are the two sweetest words in the English

language," he told me, while handing out his business card to anyone who stopped by. ISAAC'S COOKIES, they said. BAKING A DIFFERENCE SINCE 2003.

An hour and a half after we started, we were done. We had all the signatures we needed; Isaac was out of business cards; my parents were impressed; Shep was grateful; Kermit, Chad, and Baxter were chomping on a few leftover cookies; and the bake sale was declared a total success.

If only Irwin and Daisy had been there to see it.

CHAPTER 30

ON WEDNESDAY, THE night of the Zoning Board meeting, I made an announcement at dinner.

"I'm bringing Abby," I said, before my parents told me I couldn't.

My mom chuckled. "To city hall? Are you kidding?"

"I know for a fact I can bring her," I said. "When I went to see the mayor, I brought Abby. And besides, she believes in this cause just as much as I do, and we both want to fight for what we believe in!"

My dad smiled and shook his head. "Wow," he said. "It's just like that famous movie with Al Pacino. *Dog Day Afterschool.*"

"*Dog Day Afterschool?*" I asked. "Is that really a movie?"

"No," he said, "but it should be."

I nervously drummed my hand on the dining room table, thinking about presenting my petition to the board.

I'd even written a speech, and Shep told me he'd written one too. Mrs. Cragg was going to come, and maybe some people who'd adopted pets at the shelter, and other people who worked there too.

We were going to make our case, and hope for the best.

"You can bring Abby, under one condition," said my dad. "That you wear a tie."

Ack! I hated ties. And ties hated me. We hated each other. But Abby came first.

"Fine," I mumbled.

I yanked at my neck during the whole car ride downtown. Abby was looking at me like, *What is wrong with you?*

"I don't like ties," I reminded her. "We talked about this."

She cocked her head at me the way dogs do when they think you're not making any sense. Which is often.

When we pulled in to the city hall parking lot, I was surprised it was only a quarter full.

"Where is everyone?" I asked.

"People are a lot less interested in government affairs than you might think," my dad answered.

"Including us, sadly," added my mom. "I think this is the first time we've ever gone to one of these things."

I was shocked. "Seriously? That's terrible."

My dad made a guilty face. "You're right, it is."

When we walked into the auditorium though, it only took about three seconds for me to understand why it wasn't exactly the most popular game in town. There were about ten people on a stage, with one woman speaking into a microphone. She sounded the way a hypnotist might sound if they were trying to put you to sleep. The audience was made up of about twenty people who looked like they'd gotten a two-hour hall pass from an old folks' home. (Oops. I think that last comment might have been what my mom likes to call "too honest.")

"And in the matter of blah blah blah," the hypnotist was saying, "it is so ordered that blah blah blah agrees to restitution for moving his fence back blah blah without permission blah the required twenty feet blah blah that is adjacent to the property line blah."

"Welcome to town politics," said my dad.

I sat down and immediately started fidgeting. "When do we get to my petition?"

"Not sure," said my mom.

I looked down at Abby, who was lying on the floor licking one of her paws. "You're being a very good dog," I whispered to her. "Keep it up."

After five minutes—which seemed more like five hours—my dad tapped me on the shoulder and said, "Look! Another concerned citizen just showed up." I turned around to see my sister, Misty, sitting behind us with her boyfriend, Jarrod.

"Hey!" I said. "You're late."

Misty slapped me lightly on the top of my head. "Some of us actually care about finishing our homework," she said. Then she batted her eyelashes at my parents. "Especially those of us who want to get straight As so their parents reward them by letting them go on an amazing summer adventure." She was talking about that road trip with Jarrod's family.

"I'm confused," my mom said. "What part of 'over my dead body' don't you understand?"

"Ha-ha-ha-ha-ha!" said Jarrod, a little too loudly. Heads turned in his direction. "Sorry, everyone," he said. "My bad."

"I wonder where Shep and Kelsey are," I said to no one in particular. "They should have been here by now."

"I'm sure they're on their way," said my dad, but he checked his watch too.

We continued to sit there quietly while a bunch of

other people also blah blah blahed about a bunch of stuff I didn't understand. There was one interesting thing though: some guy complained that his neighbor's bird feeder was attracting hawks and vultures who were threatening his chickens, and then the neighbor said that the other guy's roosters were waking him up every morning at five o'clock. Finally, after about ten minutes of arguing back and forth, they reached a compromise: the bird feeder would be moved to the other side of the house, and the chicken neighbor would pay for a noise machine for the bird feeder guy who was getting woken up.

"Your tax dollars at work," my mom said, whatever that meant.

Finally, I heard the magic words: "And now we come to the matter of a C-1323 petition, initiated by one James Bishop, concerning the sale of 427 Main Street, and the impending closure of tenant of said building, the Northport Animal Rescue Foundation." The woman who seemed to be in charge peered down into the audience. "Mr. Bishop, are you here? Would you care to make a statement?"

Yes! And also, *Noooo!* Because where were Shep and Kelsey?

I couldn't believe they didn't show up.

I cleared my throat. "Yes, I would, Your Honor."

The woman laughed. "I'm not a judge, son, but thank you for those kind words of respect. Call me Mrs. Loeffler."

"Oh, got it. Sorry."

I walked slowly up to the microphone, which was at the front of the auditorium, near the stage.

"Thank you for allowing me to speak today. I'm here because—"

The back entrance door to the auditorium creaked open, and I breathed a sigh of relief. Backup had finally arrived!

FACT: "Backup" means reinforcements. If you watched *STOP! POLICE!*, you'd know that.

But it wasn't Shep. It wasn't even my pal Isaac, who said he might come by and try to bribe the committee with his amazing oatmeal raisin cookies (I'm pretty sure that's not legal, by the way).

Nope. It was Mrs. Cragg.

"AM I LATE?" she hollered, loud enough to wake up

all the snoozing senior citizens. "SO SORRY! I HAD TO WALK THE DOGS."

Dogs? Plural?

I felt my heart swell up with happiness when I saw her. It was amazing that she came.

It was also amazing that she brought her giant Saint Bernard, Thor, with her. She'd adopted Thor after his previous owner, Ned Swab, was arrested for sabotaging our lacrosse field and endangering the welfare of minors. (Long story. Look it up.)

But most amazing of all, she brought *another* dog! A dog that was as tiny as Thor was huge.

Mrs. Cragg and her two dogs came scrambling down the aisle, all three of them huffing and puffing.

Everyone was focused on the tiny one. "Who's this?" said my mom.

"Where are my manners!" said Mrs. Cragg. "This is Tuco, my new Chihuahua! I got him from Shep two days ago. I decided Thor needed a friend."

Tuco looked more like Thor's breakfast than his friend, but I wasn't going to say that out loud.

Mrs. Cragg leaned into the microphone. "I don't want to interrupt. I just want to add my two cents, that these

two animals are the best things that ever happened to me, and that's saying a lot, and Jimmy is absolutely right about this shelter, we cannot let it close, and besides, the last thing we need is another nail salon, or a store selling overpriced clothes!"

Tuco barked, which echoed through the whole auditorium.

"See?" said Mrs. Cragg. "He agrees with me."

She sat down.

"Thank you, ma'am," said Mrs. Loeffler. "Young man, would you like to continue with your statement?"

"Yes, please." It seemed clear at this point that Shep wasn't coming, so I just had to make the best of it and plow ahead. "The first time I went to the Northport ARF was when I adopted this dog right here. Her name is Abby, and she's a very special dog."

Abby wagged her tail and licked my nose.

"But I ended up volunteering there," I continued. "Because it's a very special place, and the guy who runs it is named Shep and he's amazing. He should be here any second." I turned to the door, one last time, but he was nowhere in sight. I looked at my parents, who signaled me to just keep going.

"I guess the thing is, animal shelters save animals, but they also save people. Because animals rescue us, just as much as we rescue them. Thank you for listening."

"That was very impressive, young fellow," said one of the men on the stage. "We will certainly take this matter under advisement."

"Please do it soon!" I begged him. "The shelter is scheduled to close next week!"

"I understand," the man said, "and we shall."

"Thank you very much."

As I walked back to my parents and Misty, who were all pumping their fists and beaming, I heard someone clapping in the back row. Everyone turned around, because you weren't supposed to clap at these things. But the person kept clapping, and when I heard her say "Go, Jimmy!" I knew exactly who it was.

Daisy Flowers.

I handed Abby's leash to Misty and ran back to Daisy. "You came!" I exclaimed. "How did you get here? When did you get here? Did you bring Purrkins?"

She shook her head. "My parents dropped me off, and they convinced me I couldn't take the chance of bringing her. What if Abby and Purrkins started fighting in front of all these people? That wouldn't look very good for the shelter."

She was right, of course.

"But I wanted to be here to support you, and your cause," she said. "Because it's my cause too. And also—I don't want us to fight anymore."

"I don't either," I told her.

And just like that, we were friends again! But two

seconds later, our brand-new re-friendship was interrupted by Mrs. Loeffler, who was trying to get my attention.

"Young man? You had mentioned that the owner of the shelter would be coming. We are about to conclude our business for the evening. Where is he?"

"He must have had an emergency," I said. "Otherwise he would definitely be here."

"Would you like to call him?"

I looked at my parents. "I have his cell number," my dad said. "Hold on."

As my dad called, Tuco was still yapping away, Abby was semigrowling at this tiny newcomer, and Thor was drooling on my mom, but we all did our best to hush. My dad was only on the phone for about a minute, but I could tell by his body language something was wrong. Finally he hung up, looking grim.

"I got ahold of Shep," he said. "I'm afraid I have some bad news. There's been a flood at the shelter. Apparently a pipe burst, and the entire facility is underwater, half the street too. The fire department is there right now." My dad paused for a second, to let that soak in. "Shep was obviously very busy and couldn't talk, so I'm afraid that's all the information I have."

Everyone was silent—even all the dogs, who could tell something very bad had just happened.

Mrs. Loeffler cleared her throat. "Well, we are all very sorry to hear that news. Obviously, we cannot hope to resolve this matter in any timely fashion until the extent of the damage is known. Our session is therefore adjourned for the evening. Good night."

We all stared at each other—the humans, the dogs, everyone. Five minutes before, it had seemed like we actually had a chance of saving the shelter. Now, it seemed like the whole thing was ruined.

"Let's go home," my mom said, finally.

But Misty didn't move. "I think we should go down there," she said.

We all stared at her, puzzled.

"To the shelter?" Jarrod asked.

"Yes!" Misty's eyes started blazing, which proved she meant business. "Let's find out what happened! Let's see if we can help! Come on!"

"Can I come with you guys?" Daisy asked. "If it's okay, I mean."

"Of course," my dad said. "Just call your mom and tell her the plan."

And just like that, we all ran out of city hall, got in our cars, and headed down to the shelter.

Our family drove right behind Mrs. Cragg. It was the first time I noticed the bumper sticker on the back of her car.

It said: DOGS ARE PEOPLE TOO.

CHAPTER 31

"WHY ARE THERE fire trucks at a flood?" I asked my parents. We were pulling onto the street where the shelter was, and there were firefighters running all over the place, and a few police cars too. It looked like the whole street was underwater.

"The fire department handles all kinds of different emergencies," my mom said. "Including getting cats down from trees."

I immediately had an image of Purrkins stuck in a tree, and Daisy crying, and me in a firefighter's hat climbing up and saving the day.

We left our dogs in our cars (with the windows half-open, of course) and started walking quickly down the block toward the shelter. No one said a word, because I think we were all in shock. Somebody had already moved most of the furniture out onto the sidewalk, and there

were some dogs and cats outside in crates. I searched for Shep but didn't see him anywhere.

"Holy moly," my dad said, under his breath. "This is crazy."

We tried to go inside, but a policeman stopped us. "Sorry, folks, you're not allowed in there," he said. "Only authorized personnel."

"I work here," I said, before realizing how silly that must have sounded.

The policeman chuckled. "Oh, you do, do you? Well, son, you need to find another job, because I think this place might have just gone out of business."

"This is hardly a laughing matter," my mom said

to the policeman. "Where are all these animals supposed to go?"

I really loved her right then.

The cop looked embarrassed. "My apologies, ma'am."

There was a sudden commotion by the door, and I turned to see Eric Miranda, the guy who worked for Mayor Murpt, coming down the sidewalk, surrounded by reporters with notepads. One of them was the woman with red hair that I'd met at city hall. I waved to her, and she waved back.

"What an unfortunate turn of events," I heard Mr. Miranda say to the reporters. "We're trying to figure out exactly what happened, but it appears that a pipe did in fact burst. This happens with some of these aging buildings, as we all know. Perhaps that's one reason this building had been scheduled for demolition and redevelopment. The important thing is to try and preserve all the businesses in the surrounding area, and of course the safety of everyone involved."

"What about the animals?" asked the red-haired woman.

Mr. Miranda smiled awkwardly. "Oh, of course, the animals too! We love all animals."

I ran up to him. "Hi, Mr. Miranda! Where's the mayor? Is she coming?"

Mr. Miranda looked down at me. "Well, hello there, Jimmy. What are you doing here?"

"I was just down at the Zoning Board meeting presenting my petition, and we heard that there was a flood."

"Isn't it awful? And after all your hard work! It's such a shame." He shook his head sadly. "Unfortunately, the mayor is at a fund-raiser for her campaign tonight, but I am keeping her informed of all developments."

"Will the mayor come here if at all possible?" asked the red-haired woman.

Eric Miranda shot her a look that was the opposite of friendly. "She is making every effort to come down here. I'll keep you informed."

The red-haired woman looked at me and rolled her eyes. "I'm holding my breath."

"Thanks for coming," said a voice behind us, and we all turned around. Shep was standing there, looking dirty, disheveled, and completely exhausted. His beloved saggy jeans were filthy, and his hair was sticking out all over the place.

We all ran up to him, saying various things along the lines of, "Shep! We are so sorry! Are you okay? This is terrible! Is everyone safe?"

"It's been quite a night," he said. "I was just getting ready to head down to city hall when I got a call from one of the nighttime security guards that water was rushing in through the back grooming area. It's pretty much been a blur ever since."

"The meeting went great," I told him, trying desperately to cheer him up. "Mrs. Cragg and Daisy came and everything. The board seemed like they were going to consider blocking the sale!"

Shep smiled sadly. "I appreciate that so much, you guys. More than you'll ever know. But I can't rebuild now. It would take too long and cost too much, even with insurance." He shook his head slowly from side to side. "It's over, Jimmy. It's over."

"NO!" I felt tears springing up behind my eyes. "It can't be!"

"What are you going to do with all the animals?" Daisy asked, and I could tell by her voice that she was trying not to cry too.

"Well, I've been thinking about that," Shep said. "I'm

going to take a page out of your book, Jimmy, and do it myself. We're going to have a big adoption party this weekend, right out here on the sidewalk, in front of the shelter."

"That's a great idea," I said.

Mr. Miranda looked up from his phone. "Normally, you'd need to apply for a permit for an event like that, but I'm sure I can talk to the mayor about making an exception in this case."

Shep nodded. "Thanks a lot," he said. "I really appreciate that."

"Can I help?" I asked.

"We'd all like to help," said Mrs. Cragg.

"You guys are so totally awesome," Shep said. "I'd love your help. Let's do this."

And in the middle of a soaked sidewalk, with firefighters running around, and dogs and cats pacing in their crates wondering what the heck was going on, and reporters writing stories about a big flood in the middle of the downtown shopping district, seven people let out a big cheer, because all was not lost.

CHAPTER 32

"HAPPY FRIDAY!" CHIRPED Ms. Owenby, two days later. "This is it! The last math test of the year!"

The class let out the biggest moan you've ever heard.

"I know, I know, it's devastating news," she continued. "But you'll just have to get over it." She started passing out the tests. "If you studied, this shouldn't be a big deal. You guys are so smart! I have faith in you." She seemed to finally be over the embarrassment of the misplaced answer sheet, and she hummed happily as she moved up and down the aisles.

FACT: If you think students get excited when the school year is almost over, you should see the teachers.

I glanced quickly in Baxter's direction. He looked sweaty. I tried to get his attention so I could give him the thumbs-up sign, but he was staring straight ahead.

"He's focusing," Irwin whispered. Even though Irwin and I were still a little mad at each other, we both wanted Baxter to do well.

"Good luck," Ms. Owenby said.

"Thanks, I'll need it," said Kermit Klondike, and everyone laughed. I laughed too, because I knew it wasn't true—it turned out Kermit wasn't just good at math, he was Irwin Wonk good.

We had forty-five minutes to do the test, but I finished in forty. It was hard, but not impossible. Ms. Owenby was right—as long as you studied, you were fine.

RIIING!!

The bell rang, and the entire class let out one big sigh of relief. No more math for the entire summer! We spilled out into the hallway, chattering excitedly. I found Baxter and Irwin, and for a minute we forgot about all the craziness that had happened over the last few weeks, and celebrated our survival together.

"We did it!" Irwin and I yelled.

"I sure hope so," said Baxter nervously.

"Let's not talk about it anymore until we get the test back on Monday," Irwin said. "Let's just enjoy the fact that it's over."

We heard a happy squeal and turned around to see Daisy flying toward us. "SO??? How'd it go?"

Irwin and I both paused, to let Baxter answer first.

"It went," he said.

"YAY!" proclaimed Daisy. I guess she was just relieved that Baxter didn't add "horrible" to the end of that sentence.

"Irwin says we shouldn't talk about it, and I'm with him," I said. Then I added, "Are you guys coming with me and Daisy to Shep's adoption party tomorrow?"

"It's going to be so much fun," Daisy said.

Irwin hesitated for just a split second, then said, "Sure."

"How about you?" I asked Baxter.

"Hold on a sec," Baxter said. "Before I answer, I have something for you."

We all looked at him, confused.

"It came a few days ago, but with studying for the test and everything, I kept forgetting to give it to you." He paused before adding, "It's from my dad."

Baxter reached into his backpack, took out a crumpled piece of paper, and handed it to me.

As I read it, my heart started to pound.

DEAR JIMMY,

MY SON BAXTER AND MY SISTER
AGNES HAVE BOTH TOLD ME WHAT
YOU'RE DOING TO TRY AND SAVE THE
ANIMAL SHELTER YOU WORK AT. I
WANT TO COMMEND YOU FOR YOUR
ACTIONS. IT IS YOUNG MEN LIKE
YOURSELF THAT GIVE PEOPLE
LIKE ME HOPE THAT I TOO CAN
CONTRIBUTE POSITIVELY TO SOCIETY
SOME DAY.

SINCERELY,
BARNABY BRATFORD

My eyes got a little watery, which I tried to ignore.
"Wow. That's kind of amazing."

"So the answer to your question is yes," Baxter said.
"I'm coming."

SATURDAY TURNED OUT to be a beautiful day for an adoption.

There wasn't a cloud in the sky as my dad and I helped Shep and Kelsey mount a giant sign outside the shelter that said, PLEASE ADOPT TODAY! EVERY ANIMAL NEEDS A HOME. Tons of people were scurrying around, moving tables and crates and cages into position, and setting up a giant ring where people could visit with the dogs or cats they were interested in. There was a pizza truck, and an ice-cream stand, and Isaac had set up a booth where he could sell his delicious cookies and cakes. All in all, everything would have been totally perfect, if not for the fact that we were doing it because the shelter was closing.

"Hey, li'l bro," said Misty, walking up to me. She had Abby, since I was working.

"Thanks for coming," I told Misty. "And for watching Abby."

"No problem!" She looked around and surveyed the situation. "Quite the doggie day care extravaganza you're pulling off here," she added. "You're turning into a pretty impressive little dude."

I stood there, shocked.

FACT: Big sisters almost never give their little brothers compliments.

"Wait a second," I said. "Did you just say something nice about me?"

Misty punched me in the arm. "Knock it off before I take it back." She pointed at her boyfriend, who was lifting a guitar case out of his car. "So, I thought Jarrod could entertain the crowd with a little music. Doesn't that sound totally cool?"

I cocked my head, which is the international symbol for *Are you serious right now?* "Jarrod plays guitar?" I asked, apparently a little too loudly, because he heard me.

"Yeah, I play guitar, what's so weird about that?" he said, punching me in the other arm. "And I sing too."

"Cool," I said. "But I should make sure it's okay with Shep."

"We'll find him," Misty said. Then she pulled on Jarrod's free hand and they strolled away, leaving me to rub my two sore arms.

I walked up to my dad. "Dad, what time is it?"

He looked at his watch. "Eleven forty-five." It was getting close—the event started at noon.

We headed over to the main table, where my job was to help check people in before they went to look at the animals. I saw Shep talking to a man in a suit. They looked like they were arguing.

My dad was watching them too. "Looks like a bank guy, or an insurance guy," he said. "Poor Shep is probably dealing with a lot of paperwork, on top of everything else."

"Can we help him, Dad?" I asked. "You work in insurance."

"*Used* to," my dad said, with a smile. "There's a reason I got out of that racket."

"Let's just find out what's going on."

My dad rolled his eyes. "Fine."

We walked over to Shep, who was saying to the guy, "I'm telling you, I don't know what you're talking about, and I don't know where it is."

"Well, that's going to be a problem," the guy said.

My dad stepped forward. "Do you gentlemen mind if I ask what it is you're discussing?"

Shep waved disgustedly at the man in the suit. "This guy thinks I did it."

My dad furrowed his brow. "Did what?"

"STARTED THE FLOOD ON PURPOSE!" Shep hollered. "For what, the insurance money?" He threw his hands up. "I don't even own the building!"

"Perhaps you had another motive," the guy in the suit said.

My dad and Shep stared at each other in disbelief.

"Here's the deal," the insurance guy said. "It wasn't a burst pipe after all. It turns out there's a piece of pipe missing and unaccounted for. A theory has emerged that would seem to indicate the pipe was removed intentionally, which caused flooding of the premises."

"Intentionally?" I repeated, not quite able to believe what I'd heard.

"That's insane," said my dad. "Completely impossible." Then he looked at Shep. "Right?"

"OF COURSE!" Shep threw up his hands. "You think I would do something like this for revenge, just because

I'm getting tossed out of here? What kind of jerk do you think I am?"

The insurance guy just stood there, looking like he'd heard it all before, which he probably had. "I'm not saying you did or didn't do anything. My job is to follow the evidence, and the evidence is telling me that someone flooded this place on purpose."

Shep looked at his watch. "Well, we'll have to continue this later, because right now we need to find some homes for these animals."

He walked away, leaving me and my dad standing there next to the insurance guy. The guy shrugged. "Well, if not him, then who?" Then he walked away too.

My dad and I looked at each other.

"Yikes," he said, which is exactly what I was thinking too.

CHAPTER 34

AS SOON AS we opened for business, there was a steady stream of customers. There were families, young couples, old couples, people of every shape and size, all looking for a pet to brighten their lives.

Irwin and Baxter were hanging out by the food trucks, of course, stuffing their faces with pizza and ice cream. I waved and they came walking over.

"Looks like it's going great," Irwin said, in between bites.

"It is," I said. I watched Baxter try to figure out a way to balance two slices of pizza and a chocolate cone. "Are you going to eat all that?"

"Why else would I be holding it?" he asked, which was a logical answer and a logical question, all in one.

I decided to be more direct. "I'm starving. Can you guys get me a slice?"

"Sure," Irwin said. "Do you have any money?"

I rolled my eyes. "Can one of you just lend it to me? What is it, a dollar?"

They looked at each other, but didn't say a word.

FACT: Best friends will do anything for you, except give you money.

"Are you guys serious right now?" I said.

Judging by Baxter's face, the answer was yes. "How do we know you'll pay us back?" he asked.

"Just forget it! My dad will get it for me!" I sat back down. "Unbelievable," I muttered, just so they knew where I stood.

"Hey, look who Daisy brought!" Irwin said, pointing and grinning.

I turned around and saw Daisy walking toward us, smiling and waving. But my eyes immediately zeroed in on what was in her hands.

Oh boy.

I was immediately reminded of the day at the Boathouse a few weeks earlier, when I also couldn't take my eyes off what was in her hands.

Because it was the same thing.

Purrkins.

"She brought the cat?" I said.

Irwin giggled. "Can't put anything past you, Mr. Detective."

I heard the sound of a man clearing his throat. I tore myself away from staring at Purrkins and noticed a man standing there with his young son. "Excuse me," he said, "may I sign in?"

"Can you give me just a second?" I asked him. "My friend just got here with her cat, and I need to say a quick hi."

The boy made a whiney face. "Come ooooonnnn!" he said. "We want to go look at the doggies! I want a doggy!"

The father made an apologetic face. "What can I say? He's been begging me for a dog for two years, and when I heard that the shelter was closing, I finally gave in and said we'd take a look and maybe get a dog."

The son looked crushed. "One? But what if we see five cute ones we want?"

The dad shook his head. "You know the drill. One dog. Maybe."

Listening to this, I smiled. It reminded me a lot of someone else who'd also come here with his dad, hoping to go home with a dog that would change his life. And that turned out to be exactly what happened.

Want to guess who that someone was?

Me.

"My friend can wait," I said. "I'll sign you in now."

I started to do the paperwork, but I was immediately distracted by the sight of Misty and Abby, heading straight for Daisy and Purrkins.

Yikes.

My heart started to beat a little louder. "Last name?" I said to the guy, hoping for a short one, so this would go faster.

"R-o-s-e-n-h-e-i-m-e-r," the guy said, so slowly it was like he thought I didn't know the alphabet. "Should you also put my wife's last name? It's different."

"We only need one," I said, so quickly it came out more like *Weonlyneedone.* I handed the sheet of paper to Mr. Rosenheimer. "Please put your phone number here, and address, and—"

I stopped talking because Misty had reached Daisy. Abby and Purrkins didn't notice each other at first, but once they did, all they did was sniff each other and check each other out. I felt a huge rush of relief.

"Where was I?" I said to the guy. "Oh yeah. Please fill this information out, and leave it right here on the table. You're all set. I hope you find the perfect dog! Thanks."

I quickly darted out from behind the table before he could think of another question, and hustled over to where Daisy and Misty were talking. Just behind them, Irwin and Baxter were finishing up their feasts.

"Hey," I said to Daisy. "I wasn't sure where you were."

"Oh!" she said. "It was a funny thing. I was halfway here before I realized that I really wanted to bring Purrkins. I mean, she came from this shelter! I wanted her to see it one last time."

"Cool," I said, even though I was pretty sure Purrkins wouldn't get much out of it. "It looks like she and Abby are getting along pretty well."

Daisy grinned. "I know! Isn't it great?"

"So great."

She turned and noticed Baxter standing there, working his way through his pizza and ice cream. "Oh man, that looks good. Where'd you get it?"

Baxter pointed toward the food trucks. "Over there."

FACT: It's a bad idea to use your hand to point, when you're holding two slices of pizza, a soda, and an ice-cream cone.

"NOOO!" Baxter hollered, as one of the pizza slices slipped out of his hand. He flailed at it, but it was no use: the slice fell to the ground, cheese side down.

"Ew, gross," said Irwin.

Abby and Purrkins stopped sniffing each other and immediately turned their attention to the fallen pizza.

I could immediately sense the growing tension in the air. "Baxter, can you pick that up before Abby gets it?" I asked. "Like, now?"

Okay, that was a bad move.

SIMILAR FACT: It's a bad idea to ask someone to pick something up if they're holding one slice of pizza, a soda, and an ice-cream cone.

As Baxter leaned down to pick up the slice, his ice cream slid off the cone and fell to the ground with a sad, wet *plop!*

"NOOOOOOOO!" Baxter hollered again, longer and louder.

Now there was a slice of pizza *and* a large scoop of ice cream up for grabs on the ground. Naturally, Abby and Purrkins both made their moves.

A WHOLE NEW FACT: Cats are quicker than dogs.

They both dashed for the ice cream, but Purrkins got there first. As she started lapping away at the melting treat, Abby turned toward the pizza, more than satisfied with cheese, sausage, and dough as a consolation prize.

The only problem was that by then, Baxter was picking up the fallen slice of pizza and depositing it in a garbage can.

Abby's eyes went cold.

She turned back to the ice cream that Purrkins was still working away on.

RELATED FACT: Cats eat a lot slower than dogs.

Abby decided she wanted Purrkins to share the ice cream.

Purrkins decided she wasn't interested in sharing the ice cream.

"GRRRRRR!" said Abby.

"HSSSSSSS!" said Purrkins.

"Misty, make sure you're holding the leash tightly," I said.

"HSSSSSSS," said Misty.

"Hi, everyone!" said Mrs. Cragg, who had just arrived with Thor and Tuco. She obviously had no idea that she'd walked right into a tense situation, but she found out soon enough, when she bent down to pet Abby and got a soft growl in return.

"Uh-oh," she said. "What's going on?"

Thor was straining at his leash, trying to get at the ice cream. Tuco started yapping away but didn't seem particularly interested in the ice cream, maybe because he weighed approximately eight ounces and wasn't hungry. I think he just thought they were all playing a game.

But it wasn't a game, it was serious business. And it was *on*.

After circling each other for about three seconds, Purrkins decided enough was enough, and she bravely jumped in front of Abby and started in on the ice cream again.

That didn't go over well.

"GRROOOWWWLL!" Abby showed her fangs and charged Purrkins, ready to tangle. Even Thor looked a little scared.

"STOP!" we all yelled, but no one was listening, especially Abby and Purrkins.

As other people turned their heads in our direction to see what was going on, Abby lunged at Purrkins, but the

cat was too quick. She decided she wasn't going to stick around to learn more about Abby's legendary fangs; she sprinted between Daisy's legs, bolted through the tent, jumped over a table, and headed straight toward downtown.

Abby took off after her, with such force that Misty dropped the leash.

"Oh boy," she said.

"Oh, great," I said.

"Oh no," Daisy said.

"LET'S GO!" I yelled, and we all sprinted after them, even though Purrkins and Abby were way faster than any of us. They were yipping and yapping and growling and howling and chasing each other, knocking into people who had come to adopt a dog or a cat (and were probably rethinking their decisions).

Three seconds later, Purrkins and Abby disappeared around a corner.

Two seconds after that, we heard a big *CRASSSSHHHH!*—and then a woman moaning.

This can't be good.

Irwin, Baxter, Daisy, and I all started running even faster, and as we rounded the corner I could barely make myself look. But somehow, I did. And I saw Abby and Purrkins with something new to fight over: a bunch of groceries that had fallen out of some woman's bag, because they had barreled into her while she was loading them into the trunk of her car—which happened to be a sweet, light-blue BMW. The woman herself was sitting on the sidewalk, her head in her hands, looking completely dazed.

I immediately picked up Abby's leash as Daisy grabbed Purrkins.

"I am so sorry!" Daisy and I said to the woman, over and over, while Baxter and Irwin tried to retrieve the various cans of food that were rolling around. Other people had followed us out of the adoption tent and were starting to gather.

"We'll buy you new groceries!" I said, which was the first thing that made the poor woman take her head out of her hands and look up.

I gasped in shock. We all gasped in shock.

It was Mayor Murpt.

I started panicking inside, wondering how this day could get any worse. This was the woman who had tried to help me save the shelter, and she had just been bulldozed by two pets who had come from that very shelter!

I had a sudden, very upsetting thought: it's possible she could have me thrown in jail for this.

"Mayor Murpt! It's you!"

"Yes, it's me," she said, barely above a whisper.

"How are you?" I said, stupidly.

That snapped her out of her shock. "How AM I? Your crazy animals nearly killed me, that's how I am!"

Mrs. Cragg walked up with her dogs. "Do you want me to hold Abby?" she asked me quietly.

The mayor's head swiveled over to Mrs. Cragg. "Who are you?" she barked.

"The babysitter," Mrs. Cragg said meekly. I think she was having bad flashbacks to the days when she almost wound up in jail herself.

"Well, I should thank you to take better care of your charges!" barked the mayor. "I could have been seriously hurt!"

By now, Shep, Misty, and Jarrod had reached us and discovered what had happened. Two seconds later, my parents came running up with horrified looks on their faces.

"Oh my goodness, what happened here?" said my mom.

"The mayor got knocked over by this dog and this cat," said some guy in the crowd, which was still growing. I guess everyone loves a good scuffle.

My mom gasped. "The mayor? Are you kidding me?"

My dad looked at me with the stare of death.

"Here are your groceries, ma'am," Baxter said, handing a ripped bag to Mayor Murpt.

The mayor slowly got to her feet. "Thank you," she said, but it didn't sound like she meant it. "You're very lucky I'm okay." She started loading the groceries into the trunk of her car, grumbling and mumbling the whole time.

It started to look like the whole thing was over, and I breathed a sigh of relief that she wasn't going to press charges or anything. Most people started to drift away, but I noticed my dad still standing there, watching the mayor. After a few seconds, he walked over to her, pointed inside the trunk, and said, "What's that?"

The mayor froze, as a few of us wandered over to take a look. I didn't know what he was referring to at first, until I saw a small thing in the corner that looked like a fat metal snake.

Mayor Murpt quickly closed the trunk. "I need to ask you to leave me alone, please. Thanks to these animals, I've had a terrible scare, and I would like to recover in peace. If you'll excuse me." She quickly walked around to the driver's side door, but my dad blocked her way.

"I'd love for you to reopen the trunk, Madame Mayor," he said.

"Are you serious?" spat Mayor Murpt. "Don't you know who I am?"

"I do," my dad said. I was trying to figure out what the heck he was doing when I noticed the insurance guy walking around behind my dad, writing something in a small notebook.

Shep stepped between my dad and the mayor. "Uh, Mr. Bishop, everything okay here?" he said. "The mayor did us a solid by letting us have the adoption party without a permit. What gives?"

My dad pointed at the car. "What gives, Mr. Lansing, is that I may have figured out what happened to your shelter." He turned his attention back to the mayor. "Please open the trunk," he repeated.

Mayor Murpt glanced around and noticed everyone was staring at her.

"I can call the police and have them do it, if you'd prefer," said my dad.

She sighed and slumped her shoulders. "Fine," she mumbled, opening the trunk.

We all peered in. It took me a second, but when I saw the defeated look in the mayor's eyes, I suddenly got it. A chill spread throughout my body as I realized what my dad was talking about. The thing in the mayor's trunk wasn't a thick metal snake after all.

It was the missing pipe.

CHAPTER 35

MAYOR MURPT'S WHOLE body sagged, like she knew the jig was up.

FACT: "The jig is up" is a popular phrase on *STOP! POLICE!* It means "You're dead meat."

The crowd was completely still and silent as my dad reached into the trunk of the car, pulled out the piece of pipe, and handed it to Shep. "I believe this belongs to you," he said.

Shep stared at the pipe in his hand. "So you're saying . . ." he began, but he couldn't bring himself to finish the sentence.

I stared at the mayor. "Is it true? You flooded the shelter? You wanted it to close all along?"

She dropped her head.

"But why?" I asked. "Why would you do such a thing?"

"I can guess," said my dad. "Would you happen to be involved in the purchase of this building?"

Mayor Murpt sat back down on the sidewalk and started to speak, so softly we all had to lean in to hear. "I am a principal investor in the company that bought the property. It was a simple transaction, the kind we do all the time, which means we had to borrow quite a bit of money to finance the purchase. We planned on paying it off when we built the shopping center." Her head slowly turned toward me. "But when this enterprising young man began his crusade to save the shelter, my partners became worried that the whole deal would fall apart, and we would be left with a giant debt to the banks. We could have lost everything. Flooding the shelter to make sure it closed for good was the only thing we could think of." She bowed her head again. "I'm very sorry. I didn't know what else to do."

My dad squatted down so he was eye level with the mayor. "We all appreciate your explanation and apology, but you should be ashamed of what you've done," he said. "And you know what? You would have gotten away with it, if not for these two animals barreling into you and stopping you in your tracks."

I looked at Abby and Purrkins, who were still panting from their adventure, and realized my dad was right.

They were heroes! Abby and Purrkins were crime-fighting heroes!

Meanwhile, two police cars had pulled up to see what was going on. My dad was nice enough to help the mayor up, and he walked her over to a police officer.

"What's going to happen to the mayor?" I asked my dad. "Is she going to jail?"

"That's for other people to decide," he said. "But her days as mayor are over, I know that much."

Irwin, Baxter, and Daisy stood there, too stunned to speak. Finally Irwin said, "Remember when we thought Kermit Klondike stole the answer sheet, and one of the reasons was because his two names started with the same letter, like Barnaby Bratford?"

I had no idea why he was bringing that up now. "Yeah, what about it?"

He grinned. "Mayor Murpt!"

I rolled my eyes.

Mrs. Cragg was trying to calm down her dogs, but she caught my eye and gave me the thumbs-up. People were rushing over to me, patting me on the back, but I couldn't really say anything. I sat down on the sidewalk, suddenly feeling really tired. So many emotions were running through my brain: confusion, shock, and disappointment at being betrayed by someone I thought I trusted.

But mostly, relief.

Shep and Kelsey walked over and sat down next to me.

"If it takes a week, a month, or a year," Shep said, "I'm keeping this place open."

I looked at him. "Really?"

"Really, little dude," he said, nodding. "I owe it to you." He pointed at everyone else, chattering excitedly. "I owe it to all of them." Then he scratched Abby behind the ear. "But mostly, I owe it to her, and all of the other animals just like her."

"That's good news!" Kelsey said. "I'm chuffed to bits!"

"You talk funny," I said, and we both laughed.

Shep and I bumped fists, and I stood up and went over to my dad. "It is important to do the right thing. But it is more important to do the correct thing."

He scratched his head. "Huh?"

"You said that to me after we accused Kermit Klondike of stealing the answer sheet," I said. "Now I get what you were talking about. You didn't make an accusation without knowing the facts. You waited until you were sure." I hugged him. "You saved the day. Thank you."

He laughed. "I knew my insurance background would come in handy some day!" Then he pointed at Abby. "But she gets the credit, along with Daisy's adorable little kitty. If it weren't for them, I wouldn't have solved anything!"

We walked over to Baxter, Irwin, and Daisy, who was cradling Purrkins in her hands. The cat looked down at Abby, and then did the perfect thing.

She yawned.

And Abby yawned back.

We all laughed.

"No wonder they're exhausted," said my dad. "It's hard work being a CrimeBiter."

"WELL, HERE WE are," said Ms. Owenby. "The moment we've all been waiting for. The moment of truth. The moment of—should I just stop blabbing on, and hand you back your tests?"

"YESSSSS!" yelled the entire class. The suspense was killing us. I think it was especially killing Baxter, who looked like he was ready to jump out the window if Ms. Owenby didn't give us our tests back soon.

"Okay," she said. "Here goes." She slowly started making her way around the classroom, handing back everyone's tests, quietly saying encouraging things like "Great job" or "Good work" or "Getting the hang of it." She got to Irwin, and I could tell by his face that he'd done really well (no surprise). Then she got to my row, and when she handed me my test she said, "Very nice performance." I looked at my grade: ninety-one. I'll take it. But believe it or not, I didn't even care that much. I had other things on my mind right at that moment.

I looked at Irwin, and we both snuck glances in Baxter's direction. We tried not to stare though, in case something bad was about to happen. But when Ms. Owenby got to Baxter, she said, "I'm really proud of you," and that was all we needed to hear. I saw a feeling of pure relief spread across Baxter's face. He looked at his test and blinked three times, as if he couldn't quite believe it.

"I got a B minus!" he yelled, over and over, as he started high-fiving everyone in sight. "I got a B minus! I got a B minus! I got a B minus!"

FACT: One man's B minus is another man's A plus.

CHAPTER 37

LET THE SUMMER begin!

As crazy as the end of the school year had been, with Baxter passing his test (yay!), and Shep getting to keep the shelter (double yay!), and Mayor Murpt turning out to be a criminal (sheesh!), and Abby and Purrkins and my dad being heroes (whoa!), the summer started with maybe the craziest news of all: my parents decided to let Misty go away with Jarrod and his family on their cross-country summer road trip after all.

I couldn't believe my ears when my parents told me.

"Seriously?" I said. "She's just a kid!"

"We trust her," my mom said. "And we trust Jarrod, and we trust his family."

"Sometimes you have to let your children have special adventures," my dad added. "It's part of growing up."

"What happened to 'over my dead body'?" I asked.

My dad chuckled. "We thought you'd be happy! Don't you want to move into her room for the summer? Wasn't that the plan?"

The truth is, I was torn. Yeah, I wanted her room. But I always got a little annoyed when Misty talked my parents into stuff, which she was really good at.

Can I tell you a little secret too?

I was worried I might miss her a little.

Let's keep that between us.

On the day they left, we all said good-bye in the driveway. Misty was kneeling on the ground, hugging Abby, while my dad was trying to lift Misty's incredibly heavy backpack into Jarrod's family's RV.

"Did you put your entire room in there?" I asked her, as we watched my dad struggle.

She grinned. "Pretty much."

FACT: Girls have a lot more stuff than boys.

"Have a great time," I said. "Don't do anything dumb."

Misty leaned over to give me a hug, and I realized that she didn't have to bend down nearly as far as she used to.

I was almost as tall as her. Pretty soon I was going to be taller!

It made me realize she wasn't the only one growing up. I was too.

That night, when my parents and I ate dinner, we were all pretty quiet. None of us talked about it, but we were all a little sad. It seemed like part of our family was missing.

"Want to go out for ice cream?" asked my dad. "Just to get out of the house?"

My mom and I both said "Yes!" immediately.

FACT: The second best cure for sadness is ice cream.

After a delicious rocky road milkshake and two episodes of *STOP! POLICE!*, it was time for bed. I was excited to spend my first night in Misty's huge room. I grabbed Abby's bed and put it in Misty's closet, because Abby likes to sleep in closets. I left the window open in case she wanted to go on one of her nighttime prowls. Then I started reading the Jonah Forrester vampire book *Fangsgiving*, which is about how Jonah helps solve the case of a criminal gang that breaks into people's houses when they're away for the holidays.

After twenty pages, I turned out the light.

"'Night, Abby," I said. She thumped her tail twice in response.

Then I lay there.

And lay there some more.

After about fifteen minutes, I realized something. I wasn't falling asleep. In fact, I was getting less tired by the minute.

I turned the light back on. Abby was staring at me. She didn't look tired either, although that was no surprise—she never seemed tired at night.

"Hey, Abby, I have an idea. Do you want to go back to our room?"

Abby was up and wagging her tail before I'd finished the question. I don't think she liked Misty's closet any more than I liked Misty's bed.

"Maybe we'll try to sleep in there tomorrow night," I told Abby, as we walked down the hall.

Once we got to my room, I put Abby's bed back in the closet, opened the window, lay my head down on the pillow, and turned out the light.

I think I was asleep in five seconds.

CHAPTER 38

"THIS MEETING OF the CrimeBiters is called to order!" Daisy announced.

It was our first summer session, and it sure was good to be back at the Boathouse. We were all there: Daisy, Baxter, Irwin, Abby, and me.

And Purrkins.

"Does anyone have any business to discuss?" Daisy asked.

"I do," I said. "But it's not really business."

Daisy nodded. "Please proceed."

I cleared my throat. "Uh, I just want to say that I'm really glad we're all back together again, and I would like to officially induct our newest member into the club." I raised my water bottle, and everyone else did the same. "Congratulations to Purrkins, and welcome to the CrimeBiters."

Everyone shouted, "WELCOME, PURRKINS!"

"If Purrkins could talk," Daisy said, "she would say that she is very grateful to everyone for understanding that sometimes it's not that easy to be the new kid, and it can be hard when things don't go well at first, and she's really happy everyone was so patient with her. So thank you." She was looking right at me when she said it.

"And if Abby could talk," I said, "she would say that she's sorry she didn't welcome Purrkins right away, but she was a little nervous about someone new coming in. But then she realized that sometimes, change is good, and now she's really glad that Purrkins is here, and she's ready for new challenges and adventures." I was looking right at Daisy when I said it.

Irwin stood up. "Well, if I could talk—which I can— I'd say that Purrkins and Abby need to stop talking, so the rest of us can get back to conducting official club business!"

Then we spent the next hour laughing, joking, making fun of each other, and doing everything except conducting official club business.

After a while, Daisy pointed out into the yard behind the Boathouse. "Look!"

We all looked. Abby and Purrkins were lying next to each other, basking in the sun. Then, when Abby got up and walked to a shady spot under an elm tree, Purrkins followed.

"That is so sweet," Daisy said.

I walked over to the animals. "You guys ready to get started with today's training?" I asked. "Everybody up! Let's go! Spin! Weave! Crouch! Lean!"

They both looked up at me.

Purrkins licked Abby's paw.

Abby sniffed Purrkins's nose.

Then they both went back to sleep.

"Sorry, Jimmy," Daisy said, "but they're doing the one thing more important than crimebiting."

"What's that?" I asked.

She smiled. "Making friends."

ACKNOWLEDGMENTS

A HUGE WOOF of thanks to all the animal shelters in the world—and the workers therein—for providing life-saving help to our most needy citizens. If it weren't for The Little Pink Shelter, my family wouldn't have Abby in our lives! And you wouldn't have this book in your hands.

ABOUT THE AUTHOR

TOMMY GREENWALD AND HIS DOG ABBY

TOMMY GREENWALD is the author of the CrimeBiters series (about a crime-fighting superhero vampire dog named Abby) and the Charlie Joe Jackson series (about the most reluctant reader ever born). Tommy lives in Connecticut with his wife, Cathy; his kids, Charlie, Joe, and Jack; and his dogs, Coco and Abby. Abby is not necessarily a crimefighting superhero vampire dog—but she makes Tommy and his family very, very happy, which is definitely a kind of superpower when you think about it. Visit him at www.tommygreenwald.com.